COUNTDOWN ZERO

CHRIS RYLANDER

COUNT ZER

WALDEN POND PRESS

An Imprint of HarperCollinsPublishers

Walden Pond Press is an imprint of HarperCollins Publishers.
Walden Pond Press and the skipping stone logo are trademarks and registered trademarks of Walden Media, LLC.

Countdown Zero
Copyright © 2015 by Christopher Rylander

Library of Congress Cataloging-in-Publication Data
Rylander, Chris.
    Countdown Zero / Chris Rylander. — First edition.
        pages cm
    Summary: "Carson Fender returns to the Agency after receiving a note in his school lunch informing him that Agent Nineteen has three days left to live, and that there might be someone inside the Agency working against them"—Provided by publisher.
    ISBN 978-0-06-212011-3
    [1. Adventure and adventurers—Fiction. 2. Spies—Fiction. 3. Middle schools—Fiction. 4. Schools—Fiction. 5. Humorous stories.] I. Title.
PZ7.R98147Cou   2015   2014022225
[Fic]—dc23   CIP
                                                                                 AC

Typography by Michelle Gengaro-Kokmen
14 15 16 17 18 CG/RRDH 10 9 8 7 6 5 4 3 2 1
❖
First Edition

For Amanda, again and always

010101010101010101010101010101010101010101010101
010101010101010000101001010101001010101010
101010000100101001010101001010101010101010
000010101010101010011001...10101
001010110101000100101...0100
101010000100101001011...CHAPTER 1...010
000010101010101010100110...101

PRANKPOCALYPSE

THE DARKNESS CONCEALED ME, EVEN AMID THE BRIGHT WHITE snow that drifted down from the night sky. I stayed low and crept behind a row of trees next to the massive brick building. The whole operation depended on the success of my next directive, which was the second phase in the mission. The third, if you count the sneaking-out-of-our-houses-after-midnight part.

I reached the window and slowly stood up, grabbing the sill and pulling myself up so I was half crouched and half sitting on the snow-covered, eight-inch-wide ledge.

1

It was about as comfortable as having two live rats fighting over a piece of cheese inside your shorts.

Not that I knew what that felt like, exactly. But it didn't matter. I wouldn't be there for very long.

I grabbed the window I'd unlocked earlier that day right after my sixth-period class. That had been phase one of the mission. I'd unlocked it from the inside and pushed it open just a centimeter when Ms. Freely's substitute teacher had stepped out to get more coffee between classes. There was no way a sub was going to check to make sure every single window was closed and locked at the end of the day. In my experience, substitute teachers were always the first ones out of there when the final bell rang. Anyway, the point is, the window was still unlocked just like I knew it would be.

The window swung open a few inches before jamming. This was something I hadn't anticipated. It could sink the entire mission. I pulled harder; the window wouldn't budge. It was only open three inches, which was not nearly wide enough for me to squeeze through.

After taking a deep breath, I pushed myself up and put all my weight onto the top edge of the window. There was a loud creak followed by a few cracking noises as the old wood and dried paint finally relented. The window popped open so quickly that I almost tumbled off the narrow window ledge and into the bushes below where I'd surely have been impaled by at least a dozen branches like some sort of all-natural, certified-organic human pincushion.

I squeezed myself through the narrow opening and, just like that, we were in business. I sent a group text to my team:

I'm in.

One of the few good things about the first snowfall in North Dakota was that it opened up a whole new array of possible pranks. Usually, this was the most exciting time of year for me. I'd spend a month deciding on the perfect prank to ring in the winter. And then I'd hammer out the details with Dillon and Danielle, who were twins and my two best friends, and we'd execute it to perfection.

But this year was a little different. This year, one prank wasn't going to be enough. Maybe it was because earlier that school year I'd become an actual, real-life secret agent and had almost single-handedly saved my town, my country, and pretty much the whole world, and since then, well, planning the same old pranks just hadn't felt like much of a challenge. Things like hiding the class hamsters somewhere in the science lab and then putting giant snakes inside their cages so that everyone would think the snakes had eaten them. (Before you get upset, know that no animals were harmed.) Actually, I'd had Dillon handle the snake wrangling. I know a lot of kids my age think snakes are cool and want one as a pet, but not me. No thanks. Snakes creeped me out worse than anything else in the world. Seriously, I'd rather wake up and find a whole nest of baby spiders hatching in my hair than have to sit three feet away from a harmless garter snake.

But, anyway, the point is that I used to think the snake/hamster prank, and any of the other ones I would pull, were hilarious. And they used to give me a big rush. Now, those pranks just weren't bringing the same sense of excitement and satisfaction that they did before the whole secret-agent thing. I was no longer Carson Fender, secret agent, codename: Zero. Even if that was a lot cooler and a lot more important, that part of my life was behind me now, and the sooner I got things back to normal, the better. I needed something major to bring me back to my real life. Hence, Prankpocalypse.

Prankpocalypse would be the largest-scale prank in the history of the world. It was going to take several hours and a lot of manpower to pull off. Which is why we had to execute it at night when no one else was around. If Prankpocalypse couldn't deliver the goods for me, then I'd probably have to face the fact that I'd outgrown pranks entirely—and a world without pranks was not one I wanted to live in. Pulling pranks was who I was. I was Carson Fender, Master Prankster. And Prankpocalypse would be my life's masterpiece. As long as it didn't get all of us expelled.

That was the main thing: to make sure nobody got caught. This was especially important today—a few of the kids in on the prank, including Danielle and Dillon, were leaving next week for a three-day field trip to Mount Rushmore that the school did for seventh graders every year. They were pretty excited about it. The two Dakotas don't really have much in the way of interesting landmarks or monuments, so Mount Rushmore was a pretty big deal for us, and the selected kids waited eagerly all year for the trip. If they got into any trouble at all, they wouldn't be allowed to go. Which explains why I wasn't going on the trip. I got into way too much trouble to be rewarded with special field trips. The school only took thirty seventh graders each year, and to qualify you needed to meet three requirements:

1. B average or better in all classes
2. Less than one hour of detention total for the whole school year
3. At least one recommendation from a teacher

I think I actually held the record for the most detention of any kid in the history of the school. That's not even mentioning my C average, or the fact that pretty much every teacher I'd had and a bunch that I didn't disliked me for one prank or another. I was bummed, of course, because it'd be fun to miss a whole day of school to go on a camping trip with Dillon and Danielle. But there wasn't much I could do about it now. Anyway, it made secrecy the number-one concern while executing Prankpocalypse.

I exited the classroom and switched on my flashlight. The empty school hallways looked a lot creepier at night. I found myself thinking of all of those scary movies I'd seen and wishing I hadn't seen them. Thankfully, the need to focus on the mission at hand kept me from turning around and sprinting right back down the hall and out the window I'd just entered.

There was a side door by the gym that was one of the few in the school that could be unlocked from the inside without a key. Most of the main entrances were these huge glass jobs that required a key, even from the inside. But this particular door could be opened simply by pushing the lever.

My crew was outside waiting with nervous grins on their faces.

"You guys ready?" I asked.

"Are you kidding?" said Jake, our newest prank recruit. "Let's do this thing."

Jake had always been on the fringes of our group of friends, but this was his first time in the inner circle. I could tell he was the most nervous and excited of all of us, likely from an adrenaline high. That can happen when pulling your first prank. While it was definitely risky to let a rookie in on Prankpocalypse—especially one whose mom was on the school board—this was no ordinary prank, and we needed the manpower. Plus, Dillon had really taken a liking to Jake and insisted he was a good guy whom we could trust.

"Settle down, Jake, jeez," Danielle said. "You're gonna have a heart attack before we even get started."

Danielle hadn't been as excited as her brother about letting Jake help us out. She said Prankpocalypse was too important to put even a small piece of it in the hands of a newbie. But I had a feeling it was more than just his inexperience. Even I could see that Danielle didn't like him as much as the rest of us did. I couldn't figure out why, but then, girls always seemed to dislike random kids for no reason.

Either way, I laughed and moved aside so the whole crew could enter: Dillon, Danielle, and Jake, followed by Zack, Ethan, Katie, and Adie. They carried backpacks filled with supplies, except for Zack, who pushed in a giant wheelbarrow containing several plastic sleds and a few small snow shovels. That honor had been his, since he lived closest to the school.

The basic concept behind Prankpocalypse was pretty simple: execute as many pranks at the same time as humanly possible.

But the execution of it was a lot more complex than that. For one thing, it was already past midnight, so we probably had less than four hours before we ran the risk of being spotted near the school. Second, most of the school classroom doors operated on automatic locks, which meant they were always locked when closed. This limited most of our pranks to the common areas.

Here's a small taste of what we had planned for Prank-pocalypse:

- Build a huge wall of snow behind every entrance of the school (to be completed last to reduce melting time)
- Rearrange all the sauce and condiment bottles in the cafeteria (i.e., put mustard in the ketchup bottles, hot sauce in the mayo bottles, etc.)
- Hide all the tables and chairs in the cafeteria and common areas inside one of the school bathrooms
- Cover the floors completely with printed pictures of animals pooping (this one had been Jake's idea; Danielle found it pretty gross and stupid, but the rest of us agreed that it was hilarious, and so it stayed in)
- Cover as many windows in black paint as possible
- Hide expired eggs all over the school

The main event, though, was a special prank I had planned specifically for Principal Gomez's office. This was one I'd be taking care of personally, as it would require some pretty serious lock picking, which was something I'd learned how to do during my secret-agent training. I'd never actually done it in the field, but I had been keeping my skills sharp at home using a lock-picking kit I bought online. Once inside his office, I was going to build a giant snowman replica of Principal Gomez behind his desk. I'd even brought a fake stick-on mustache and a terrible fur scarf I found at Salvation Army that looked remarkably similar to his scrappy hair.

I know that it probably sounds like I'm pretty hard on old Mr. Gomez—that, in fact, all of this might be considered mean-spirited by outside observers. And I agree, it would be really mean—that is, if Mr. Gomez didn't absolutely deserve it.

It's not as if he was a terrible principal or an outright evil human being; as far as I knew he wasn't secretly killing baby birds at lunchtime and keeping their carcasses stored in his small office fridge like some kind of sadistic trophy case (or, at least, I hoped not). It's more that he was simply just a jerk. Hardly anybody liked him. Even the teachers sometimes mumbled and grumbled things under their breath about Principal Gomez and all his crazy rules. Some examples of his inhumane mandates:

- Students were not allowed to doodle in their notebooks. Ever. If they did, it was an automatic detention. Gomez would actually go as far as stopping kids in the hallway to spot-check their notebooks for evidence of doodling.

- Students were required to tuck in their shirts at all times. Our school didn't have uniforms or a strict official dress code or anything like that. It didn't even matter what kind of shirt you were wearing. I mean, have you ever seen a football jersey tucked into shorts? Or a sweater tucked into jeans? Yeah, didn't think so. Trust me, it was ridiculous.
- Bathroom hall passes were restricted to just three per week per student. I don't even need to explain why that one was crazy.
- Organized games were not allowed during the leftover time at lunch period. That meant no football, kickball, tag, Magic cards, or any other such activity. All we could do was sit outside, or stay sitting inside the cafeteria. Which was of course just what every kid wanted during a long school day: more sitting.

There were more, but I'm getting too mad even listing these ones to continue without getting a nosebleed. Thankfully, very few teachers enforced many of these rules. You'd likely only get busted if Gomez himself caught you breaking them. Which just goes to show how ridiculous the rules were, that he couldn't even get the teachers to enforce them. The way I saw it, these pranks were just sweet, sweet justice.

Anyway, while the rest of my crew set about pulling their assigned pranks, I picked Gomez's door lock with surprising ease, and a couple hours later I was putting the finishing touches on the finest snowman I'd ever built. It looked about as much like Gomez as was possible for being constructed out of frozen water. I was standing there, admiring my work, when my phone vibrated. It was a text message from Dillon.

Gomez just pulled up! Get out of there!

0101010101010100001010100101010100101010101010
1010100001001010010101010010101010101010
0000101010101010100110010101010101
0010101101010001001010100
101010000100101001010
00010101010101010011

CHAPTER 2

SOMETIMES IT *IS* LIKE IN THE MOVIES

THE DIGITAL CLOCK ON MY PHONE READ 2:53 A.M.

I reread the text message, just to make sure I wasn't seeing things. Gomez should be home sleeping like a normal human being. Right?

I quickly switched off my flashlight and peeked out the office window.

Sure enough, Gomez was striding up the sidewalk toward the school, fully dressed, as if he always arrived at work at three o'clock in the morning. I admit I hadn't checked to see if anyone arrived before 4:00 a.m. Gomez had showed plenty of signs of insanity in the past, so this was a major error on my part.

Also, there was a good chance he'd seen the light from my flashlight in his office window when he pulled up because he was looking my way and walking incredibly fast, even for him.

I quickly texted a reply:

Just make sure everyone else gets out.

I looked out the window again, but Mr. Gomez was gone. He was likely already inside the building. The office was just twenty or thirty feet from the front entrance, which meant I had less than a minute to get out of there. It was too bad we hadn't walled off that entrance with snow yet.

Gomez was just entering the administration area outside his office door as I glanced at the sled still on the floor with the leftover snow piled on it. We were all wearing winter gloves so I could probably leave that behind without worrying about anyone finding something with my fingerprints on it. Leaving behind evidence of any kind was not ideal, but I had bigger concerns right then.

There was really only one possible escape route left: Gomez's office window.

I scrambled behind his desk and fidgeted with the

latch. It wouldn't budge. It probably rarely got opened. Gomez didn't strike me as the sort of guy who relished fresh air. In fact, it sometimes seemed like the stuffier a room felt, the more comfortable he was. Like he was some sort of creepy cave-dwelling creature that enjoyed lurking in dank environments and eating bat droppings, instead of being just a normal old principal who liked comfortably conditioned indoor rooms.

There was a click as Gomez slid his key into the lock.

It was too late. I was finished. A former secret agent taken down by a middle school principal. That was pretty embarrassing. Not that I was going to just give up and stand there sheepishly as I got caught. No way would my secret-agent mentors, Agent Nineteen and Agent Blue, give up that easily. So neither would I.

As Gomez unlocked the door, I dived behind a huge file cabinet and pressed myself up against the wall. It was a terrible hiding spot since he would easily see me if he stepped around to the far side of his desk for any reason. But it would at least buy me a few seconds to think.

After another moment fidgeting with the knob, Gomez was inside. His office was tiny, so I breathed as slowly and quietly as I could. But I didn't need to worry about being quiet—as soon as Gomez saw the state of his office and the snowman version of himself behind the desk, he lost it. He puffed and sputtered, completely speechless.

"Aaarrgh!" he finally shouted, all piratey.

I stifled a laugh. Even in this dire situation, I couldn't help but think of Gomez's bulging eyes carefully examining his snowclone. But that didn't mean I had stopped brainstorming ways to get out of the office without Gomez noticing.

My coat pocket vibrated. Holding my breath, I slowly pulled out my phone. It was another text from Dillon:

Did you make it out?

I debated typing a reply but realized that I could no longer hear Gomez. Was he still there, not making noise? Or had he stepped out? Was it worth poking my head around the corner of the file cabinet to check? I put my phone back into my pocket and listened for breathing.

There was nothing audible but my own shallow breath, which sounded to me like a chainsaw trying to cut through a slab of marble. I leaned to the side slightly until I could see through the door. Gomez wasn't out in the main office where the school secretary sat. But I did see him in the reflection of the office door's window.

He was still inside his office, next to the desk, digging

in his briefcase for something. If I could see him, that meant he'd be able to see me back in the reflection if he happened to look at the office door closely enough. I needed to act.

I reached into my coat pocket and pulled out a black stone I had brought for the Gomez snowman's eyes. I checked the reflection in the door. Gomez still had his head down. I'd only have one chance at this and I'd have to move fast.

My plan wasn't a good one. Actually, it was pretty bad. In fact, it was more likely to result in a broken neck or severed artery than a safe exit. And in that regard, it was maybe the worst plan I'd ever come up with in my whole life. Perhaps even the worst plan that anyone had ever come up with in the history of plans. But then again, it was the only one I had. Besides, I had faced down a small army of trained terrorists with automatic weapons just a few months ago. If I could do that, then surely I could escape from a middle school principal's office.

I took a deep breath and leaned to the side again, so I could just see the open office door. The target was small, and I wasn't exactly Aaron Rodgers, but it wasn't very far away either.

My windup was hindered by the small space, but I

put as much power into the throw as possible. The small black stone fired from my hand with surprising speed and shot through the open door.

It smashed into the secretary's desk, knocking a cup full of pens and pencils off the edge with a crash. Gomez leaped up from his chair with a cry. I heard him slam into the snowman.

He cursed. I did, too, silently. He'd just killed my poor snowman that had taken over an hour to construct.

I stayed hidden as he ran from his office trailing chunks of snow into the main administration area. As soon as he was clear of the door, I sprang out from behind the file cabinet, pulling the second Gomez eye rock from my pocket and firing it at the window behind his desk.

A small, jagged opening appeared in the glass, with cracks spreading around it like a spiderweb. I could only hope the small hole had greatly reduced the strength of the entire windowpane. But I didn't have time to wonder about it any longer, because Gomez was likely already on his way back toward the office.

I lunged forward in three long, quick steps and dived headfirst with my elbows out in front of me toward the center of the window. I half expected to bounce off it and end up on my butt back inside Gomez's office, staring up at his blazing red eyes with my neck bent at an awkward angle. But the weakened glass gave way and I plowed right through the window and into a snow-covered bush just outside. The padding of my winter coat helped me avoid getting stabbed or cut by shards of glass or the bush's branches.

After I landed, I didn't stop to see if I'd broken any limbs. I immediately rolled to my right and then took off sprinting along the side of the school building.

As I reached the end of the building and turned the corner sharply, I heard Gomez shouting from the hole in the window.

"I see you! I *know* who you are!"

His words faded behind me as I ran.

He likely did know it was me. But the cold fact was that he couldn't prove it. Would he find a reason to give me a ton of detention, like usual? Yeah, definitely. Would he have enough evidence to actually expel or suspend me? Nope. He never did.

I grinned as I ran toward our rendezvous spot. Prankpocalypse had gone off about as well as one could expect, all things considered. To be honest, though, I was a bit surprised at how little I was looking forward to the morning-after payoff. That used to be my favorite part.

As I ran through the silent North Dakota snowfall, all I could think about was the thrill at almost getting caught and the rush of the escape.

Of course, if I had known then what I was going to find in my lunch the following week, I might not have been craving so much excitement after all.

1010101010101010100110010101010101010101
01010101010100001010010101010010101010100
10101000010010100101010010101010101010101
00001010101010101001100░░░░░░░░░░░101010
0010101101010001001░░░░░░░░░░░░░░░100:
1010100001001010010░░░░░░░░░░░░░░░010:
00001010101010101001100░░░░░░░░░░░1010

CHAPTER 3

SECRET CORNED-BEEF MESSAGES FROM REFORMED PIRATES

MOST KIDS PROBABLY DON'T EXPECT TO FIND A SECRET MESsage hidden in their school lunch.

If they did, they'd probably think someone was playing a joke on them or something. Or, if they were anything like my conspiracy-theorist best friend, Dillon, they'd probably assume that the secret message was from a member of the League of Reformed Pirates trying to rally support for their fight to get more realistic glass eyeballs so they don't freak people out when they get tired of wearing their eye patches.

But when I found a top secret message in my corned beef the Wednesday after the smashing success that was Prankpocalypse, I most certainly did not think it had come from the League of Reformed Pirates. In fact, I knew exactly who had sent me the secret message before I even read it.

At the same time, I didn't know what the slimy, gravy-covered slip of paper was going to say. But I certainly wasn't expecting it to deliver a blow so devastating that I'd feel like I'd just gotten kicked in the jaw by a farm mule named Arnold who was juiced up on steroids and spent fourteen hours a day pulling heavy carts around his pen.

Agent Nineteen has seventy-two hours to live. Meet on the school track in six minutes.

I couldn't keep my hand from shaking. I looked up and found Dillon staring at me.

"What's wrong?" he asked.

"Nothing," I said. "I just have to go save the world again."

My name is Carson Fender, and just in case you're con-fused by all this "secret agent" talk: A few months ago I saved the world. Well, sort of. The thing is, being a real secret agent isn't always like it is in the movies. There wasn't some maniacal evil genius who had a disintegration laser pointed at the earth's core, or a secret satellite he'd rigged to blow up the moon. No, in real life, fighting villains and saving the world is more complicated than that.

So, maybe I didn't stop the earth's core from being destroyed or prevent the moon's destruction or anything. But I did help to take down an evil organization called the Pancake Haus (don't ask) and stop them from freeing several dangerous terrorists from prison and just generally wreaking havoc across the globe.

And, yeah, so maybe I didn't exactly take them down completely. Their leader, Mule Medlock, got away and is still out there somewhere, likely concocting a new scheme of some sort. But I still helped to capture most of his henchmen and put a pretty big dent in his organization's structure and plans. I'm not bragging. It was probably more luck than anything. Besides, it was kind of my own fault that Mule Medlock even got as close as he did to succeeding in the first place.

But all of that is a long story and beside the point. That all happened months ago. And since then I'd been retired from the Agency. They didn't need my help anymore, and I hadn't received any official Agency messages since the night that stuff all went down.

And now, suddenly, this. A note in my corned-beef casserole telling me that the man who recruited and trained me, Agent Nineteen, was about to die, and that, for some reason, the Agency thought I could help save him.

I excused myself from the table.

"What do you mean 'save the world'?" Dillon asked. "Where are you going?"

"Look, I gotta go . . . uh, you know . . . go to the bathroom," I said. "I just call it 'saving the world' sometimes."

Dillon grinned. "I like it! That sounds a lot better than what I usually say, which is, 'I gotta go feed the fish.' Or sometimes I say, 'I have to go release the kraken' or 'drop anchor.' Every once in a while I say, 'I gotta go plan the dictator's assassination.'" He paused. "'I have to go save the world.' Yeah, I like it!"

"Great, you get him started and then take off and leave the rest of us with the results?" Danielle said. "Both of you are utterly twisted and disgusting."

"Sorry, duty calls," I said, hurrying away before they could distract me any longer.

Several kids tried to stop me to tell me their Prank-pocalypse stories. That had been happening a lot since the night we'd pulled it off: Almost every kid had some funny story relating to one of our many pranks that night. Normally I'd have loved to just stand around talking about the hilarious success of one of the pranks, but instead I just brushed them off with a quick fist bump. Because right then I needed to get down to the school track. Agent Nineteen was in trouble; I didn't have time to waste talking about secret bathroom codes or trivial pranks.

There was something much more important in the works now.

0101010101010101010101010101010101010101
01010101010101000010100101010100101010101010
1010100001001010010101010010101010101010
000010   0011001010101010101010101
0010   0010101010010101010100
101   1010100101010101010
000   1100101010101010101010101

CHAPTER 4

WIZARD VS. ARMADILLO

THERE WAS ONLY ONE PERSON WAITING FOR ME DOWN BY THE school track: Agent Blue.

Agent Blue was Nineteen's partner and my other mentor when I'd been an almost agent earlier that year. Agents Blue and Nineteen were also Mr. Jensen and Mr. Jensen, teachers at my school, and they did a pretty good job at playing the parts.

"Carson," he said stoically.

"I got your message."

He nodded solemnly. Neither of us needed to say much more about it.

"It's imperative we don't waste any time," he said. "I've already arranged for you to miss your next class. We need you to come down to HQ right away."

I nodded, figuring there would be time for all the questions I had later. I followed him toward the old shed by the sledding hill, which housed the secret entrance to Agency Headquarters.

I'd only ever been to the Agency HQ one other time. It was right after I'd saved my friend, the kid I'd been assigned to protect, Olek, from the Pancake Haus. But that didn't mean I hadn't thought about it every day since then. I mean, there was a massive secret base miles underneath our school, where dozens of people did top secret things, and all while we lived our relatively boring lives up above them, completely unaware of how much was being done to *keep* our lives as boring as possible. After all, for many people, excitement isn't always a good thing.

But the point is, how could I not think about that stuff all time? It almost made me wish I didn't even know about the Agency or their secret headquarters at all, because it basically drove me crazy to think about what they were doing while I was taking some meaningless social studies quiz or changing into my gym clothes or waiting for the school bus. And the worst part was that I couldn't tell anyone about it. There was nobody I could talk to about the secrets I knew.

For those first few weeks, I'd been so consumed by the knowledge of the Agency's existence that Dillon and Danielle would catch me just standing there staring at the ground for minutes at a time. Dillon of course had merely assumed that I was only shocked to see what he himself had discovered during the past few weeks: that an army of mutated, hyperintelligent ants were plotting something massive at our school, something that involved kids being carried away into secret ant lairs to be turned into ant slaves or ant food or maybe just experimented on with a complex and varied array of ant tools by psychotic ant scientists.

Danielle's concern was a bit simpler. At first she'd just figured that I missed Olek. She had known Olek as nothing more than a foreign exchange student, and we'd all become pretty good friends in the short time I had been assigned to protect him. Her theory was partially true. I did really miss Olek since he'd returned to living with his family. But missing Olek didn't cause me to stare at something for five minutes straight with a look on my face like I thought I'd just seen a wizard sword fighting an armadillo but wasn't quite sure if I'd really seen it or was just losing my mind. And that's why Danielle started to think something else was wrong.

"What's with you lately?" she'd say after noticing me gazing.

"I'm telling you, he sees the Einstein ants, too!" Dillon would shout, crouching on the ground to get a closer look.

Danielle would always ignore him while I tried to cover for myself, making up some lame lie or another.

But the truth was, it was getting increasingly tougher not to just come clean entirely. To tell Dillon and Danielle the actual truth: that I had been a real secret agent for a few weeks earlier that year, and that pretty much half of Dillon's insane theories about our hometown were actually true (you know, all the ones that didn't involve superintelligent ants and the like). They were my best friends, after all. If I couldn't trust them with my biggest secret, then who could I trust?

But in the end, I always kept my mouth shut, because of something Agent Nineteen had said to me once: *Forget all the rules of being a secret agent that movies might have told you. The first and only steadfast rule to being an agent is: Don't ever blow your cover. Ever. That's when people start dying.*

I stood outside the maintenance shed while Agent Blue input all the secret codes and had his retinas scanned by a security device. A moment later we were on the hidden elevator that doubled as the floor of the shed. We zoomed down into the earth, and just like last time it felt like it took my stomach an extra forty seconds to join us at the bottom.

The scene before me when the elevator opened, though, was nothing like last time. Then, the office had been pristine and professional, with men and women in sharp suits efficiently monitoring hundreds of cameras and text feeds coming in from around the world, a well-oiled machine of modern surveillance and espionage.

As soon as the doors parted this time, I found myself staring down the barrels of four huge machine guns.

My first thought was that Blue and I had been ambushed. My next thought, a split second later, was that Agent Blue had just led me into a trap as part of some cruel training exercise. My third thought, fueled by the terror of having real guns pointed my way, was that I wished I'd brought a change of pants.

"Security clearance?" said a voice.

"Zulu-tango-nine-four-four-zulu-oscar-lima-seven," Agent Blue said calmly, as if having four machine guns pointed at his face were as boring and routine as ordering an Egg McMuffin at the drive-thru on his way to work in the morning. "Guest access: alpha-juliette-six-six-zero, per directive one-four-seven-five-eight-eight."

Just like that, the guns were lowered and the four men in full body armor and riot masks stepped aside and let us pass.

"What was that all about?" I said as we entered the lobby, the huge atrium that made up the heart of the Agency Headquarters. The last time I had been down here it had been packed with Agency employees and bustling with activity. Now it was oddly empty and quiet, virtually deserted.

"Discovering there's a rogue agent on the loose can cause a lot more havoc than you might think," Agent Blue said.

"You mean Medlock?" I said. The psychotic criminal

mastermind I'd met earlier that year had once been an agent with this very organization. It's one of the reasons he was able to wreak such chaos with his plan. He knew exactly who he was fighting, and what each of the Agency's moves would be. Including hiring me.

Agent Blue nodded. "I guess it's a good lesson in who you can really trust." He paused as we ascended the glass steps leading up to the HQ offices, and then added while shaking his head, "You never really can know who your true friends are."

I swallowed, and thought again about Dillon and Danielle. About how Medlock and Nineteen and Blue had apparently all once been friends and partners who trusted one another completely. And about how close I'd come to telling my own friends my secret just four days ago when we'd all gone to see the newest James Bond movie together.

The difference, of course, was that my friends were just harmless seventh graders, whereas Mule Medlock, aka Agent Neptune, had been a highly trained secret agent who was somehow still alive despite the fact that Agent Nineteen had seen him get shot in the head while out on a mission. Getting shot in the head had to mess a person up at least a little bit. It's not like my friends would ever go crazy and cause some huge national security crisis like Medlock.

Not even Dillon would do something like that.

CHAPTER 5

THE GUTS STEW QUESTION

AGENT BLUE LED ME TO AN EMPTY CONFERENCE ROOM AND told me to have a seat at a large table.

"Wait here," Agent Blue said, and left the room before I could even say anything.

I'd forgotten in the last few months just how frustrating it could be, working with the Agency. Everything was always on a "need to know" basis with them, which meant that I was often kept in the dark about things until someone decided to tell me, and what questions I could ask were often met with silence, or a question in return, or even worse, a short, cryptic answer that really only left you with even more questions than you had to start with. So I just sat there and tried not to think of more questions to add to my growing list.

It seemed like it took hours for Agent Blue to come back. When he finally did, he took a seat across from me.

"Is Medlock behind this?" I asked before he could say anything. "Did he capture Nineteen?"

"We aren't sure," he said. "The issues the Agency has been dealing with lately are almost certainly related to security leaks, but we don't have any hard evidence that Medlock himself is behind any of it. In fact, he's virtually disappeared since the incident at the circus earlier this year. That said, it'd be foolish to assume that he's simply gone away or that any of the recent oddities are completely unrelated. Here at the Agency, we're not allowed to believe in coincidence."

I nodded slowly. I decided to keep my other fifty-seven questions to myself and just let him talk. He wouldn't have brought me all the way down here, during school, to sit across from me and not say anything.

"It started with a few missing field agents," Agent Blue

began. "That's a rare-enough occurrence, and unquestionably cause for alarm. Hence the extra security you must have noticed."

I nodded.

"From there, things have only gotten worse," he continued. We shared a look, and he didn't even need to mention Nineteen's name. I realized that, despite his completely blank exterior, he was just as confused—and perhaps even as frightened—as I was. "But before I get into all that, I need to ask you, straight out, if you're prepared to come work for us again."

I'd suspected that was why I was brought down here, but officially hearing it spoken aloud still carried with it a wave of shock and excitement. The same sorts of feelings I used to get executing perfect pranks.

"I want you to truly consider the question before answering," Agent Blue said, his dark tone carrying a surprising edge. "Because this isn't going to be like last time. When we asked for your help in protecting Olek, there was the possibility of danger, of course, but you were never intentionally put directly into harm's way by any of your Agency directives. This time . . . will be different."

He let that part linger for a few seconds before continuing.

"I'm going to be blunt, Carson: What we're about to ask will put you in a situation not dissimilar to that of a trained and experienced field agent, and will carry with it all the same risk, both to your person and to the Agency. We think you can help us save Agent Nineteen's life; we wouldn't be sitting here otherwise. But you need to know what you're getting into."

I let the question sink in. It felt as if it just melted into me like acid, burning my skin and bones and heart and lungs. The question seeped into my guts and melted them into a kind of gross blood and organ stew with my stomach acting as the stockpot.

And then I considered my options. It basically broke down like this:

1. I could say yes and maybe get killed. Or maybe I would save the day and save the world again, and most importantly save Agent Nineteen.

2. I could say no and then carry with me the knowledge that if Agent Nineteen died, it would be partly my fault for not even trying to save him. If I ever even found out what happened to him, that is, which was

unlikely given the Agency's love of secrets—and perhaps never finding out would be even worse.

3. I could say nothing, just sit here and stall for as long as possible, while the seconds in Agent Nineteen's life slowly ticked away.

To be blunt, all of the options sucked. It's easy to dream of being a secret agent, but another thing entirely when you're confronted with the reality of what it might mean. Add this to the fact that every minute I thought about it was a wasted one. There were less than seventy-two hours left in Nineteen's life according to the slip of paper in my corned beef, and I was wasting those precious minutes by sitting there debating whether or not to help save him.

And then something else occurred to me. For some reason, at that moment, I thought about Prankpocalypse. About how much I had pretended to love it as much as my friends. If the failure of Prankpocalypse to really bring back the excitement of my old life meant anything, it meant that maybe I was meant for something more than just running around with my friends at three in the morning giving my principal a hard time.

"I'm in," I said.

Agent Blue must have seen the look on my face as I'd

debated the question. He must have seen how tough it was to make such a decision with so little information. And he must have seen the conviction in my response.

Because instead of questioning me further or asking me if I was really sure, he simply nodded, and said, "Let's go meet the Agency director."

0101010101010000010100101010100101010100
1010100000100101001010100101010101010101
00001   0011001010101010101010
0010   0010101010010101010100
101   1010100101010101010101
100   1100101010101010101010

CHAPTER 6

BONECRUSHER AND THE ZOMBIE APOCALYPSE

AGENT BLUE POKED HIS HEAD OUT THE DOOR OF THE CONFER-ence room and looked both ways before we exited. I followed him as he walked quickly along the wall opposite the glass railing surrounding the Lobby balcony. Seeing him sneaking through his own Agency's workplace like an outside spy made me even more nervous than I already was.

At the end of the walkway stood a wall of solid concrete. Agent Blue stopped next to it and then pressed his palm against the hard surface. The wall slid aside, revealing a short metal hallway. We stepped inside and the concrete slab slid shut.

After one more set of secure doorways with retina and fingerprint scanners leading down another short hallway, we were finally inside of a massive office. It had large glass computer monitors everywhere and two huge desks. Behind one of them sat a man so large that he made the wooden desk look like a stepping stool.

He nodded at us as we entered. "Welcome."

Agent Blue and I sat in chairs across from the freakish monstrosity.

"Carson, this is Director Isadoris," Agent Blue said as we sat.

In movies, the Agency director or head of the division or whatever is usually some scrawny old guy with thinning gray hair, steel-rimmed glasses, and a cool and calculating manner. Or sometimes it is a bearded fellow with a sly grin and a gruff demeanor, but kind eyes that sparkle with a razor wit and years of hard-earned wisdom. Or something. It definitely usually isn't a massive, hulking middle-aged dude who looks like he belongs in a UFC cage fight and has a nickname like Bonecrusher that he earned after literally crushing his opponent's bones into powder during a match.

"My friends call me Bonecrusher," Director Isadoris said with a grin, extending his meaty paw across the table.

My jaw flopped open. Then he chuckled and removed a thin metal disc that had been attached to his head. He set it aside.

"My nickname's not really Bonecrusher," he said. "I was just testing a new device our PTD team has been working on. My apologies."

"That thing reads minds?" I said weakly.

"In a way," he said, but he didn't expand on that, and I was too stupefied to ask. "Let's start over. I'm Director Isadoris."

He held out his hand again. It was easily the size of my whole head. I shook it. Nothing had ever made me feel smaller in my life.

"I'm Carson . . . or, uh, Agent Zero."

He grinned, but only for a moment. "Yes, I think we can reactivate your file and codename, given the dire circumstances. I know we didn't have a chance to meet during your last stint with the Agency, and that was likely for the best. Still, I was quite impressed with your work, and Agents Nineteen and Blue expressed as much in their field reports as well. Despite your lack of experience, they were convinced that Olek would have been compromised without your help. Which brings me to why you're here." He took a file from the corner of his desk and opened it in front of him. "Last weekend, Agent Nineteen traveled to a remote base of ours for a routine check-in. Shortly after his arrival, one of our automated security sensors transmitted an abnormal reading. It seemed like it was nothing important at the time, likely just a technical glitch. But a few hours later, it became clear that something more serious had occurred."

He paused. Agent Blue's head was down and his hands were clasped tightly in his lap.

"What happened?" I asked.

"This particular base's primary directive involves the research and production of insidious biochemical agents," Director Isadoris said.

"Like, germ warfare or something?" I asked. I'd played enough video games to know what he was referring to.

"In a manner of speaking, yes," Director Isadoris said. "Some of the Agency's activities might appear *aggressive* to an outside observer. But part of biochemical prevention and preparedness is knowing what the enemy may do or use before they even do themselves." He leaned forward, towering above me.

"And one of the biochemical agents, or whatever, got released inside this base?" I ventured.

He nodded.

Nineteen had already explained earlier that year that being a Chaos Breaker (which is what Agency personnel sometimes informally called themselves) meant doing things that might seem pretty scary or even outright wrong on the surface. It didn't come as any surprise to me that the Agency had created the virus that was threatening Agent Nineteen's life at that moment.

"We're not sure exactly what caused the outbreak in the lab," Director Isadoris continued. "The base's automated remote-communication link remained active just long enough for us to determine that a prototype airborne virus codenamed Romero had, in fact, been released in some capacity within one of the base's science labs and possibly elsewhere within the facility. A very short time later, we lost contact with the base entirely. That was two days ago."

"How do you even know any of them are still . . . ," I started, before fear that Agent Nineteen might already be dead choked off my last few words.

"We don't know," Director Isadoris said. "But the Romero Virus only remains active for twenty-four hours after its release. It is highly potent and contagious, though. Once a person is infected, the virus slowly consumes the body's nervous system, including the brain. In layman's terms, the virus essentially causes the brain cells to literally eat themselves. Fortunately, we do believe that the virus has been contained within the base. Its structure was specifically designed to prevent exterior breaches should such a *situation* ever occur."

I shifted in my seat and tried not to think about Agent Nineteen's brain eating itself to death.

"How do you know it didn't get out?" I asked.

"The laboratory wing of the base is completely air locked at all times, and if that air lock is breached without authorization, it sets off a remote security alarm signal. If anyone tried to enter or exit the lab areas without proper clearance, we'd know about it."

"But you don't know for sure," I said. "What if someone with authorization sabotaged the lab?"

Director Isadoris stiffened. "That's precisely why we're here. Given that we don't know who we can trust anymore, we need your help. Your mission will be to infiltrate the base, deliver the antidote, rescue any agents trapped inside, and, most important, help ensure that what's left of the virus does not get outside the base. Even if that were to mean destroying both the virus and the base itself."

"Destroy the whole base?" I asked, not sure I'd heard him correctly.

"Yes, one option for us at this point would be to use a covert radio signal to initiate the Base Security Breach Self-Destruct Sequence. But, as the name might give away, that would not be the best possible outcome for Agent Nineteen or any of the others still trapped inside. And we don't anticipate the need for you to initiate the sequence, either. But it's certainly a possible outcome, if the outbreak ends up to be worse than we suspect."

I just sat there and gaped at Director Isadoris, and the same questions from last year flooded my brain. *Why me? Wouldn't a team of highly trained adult agents be much more effective than a thirteen-year-old retired part-time sort-of agent?* I was too shocked and confused for my mouth to function enough to ask this question.

"You're probably wondering why you," Director Isadoris said. I glanced at the mind-reading device sitting on the desk. He followed my gaze and smirked momentarily. "This whole situation *must* remain completely covert. In order to get the trapped agents out, you'll need to release the outbreak security hatches, which can't be triggered from inside the lab, where most of the staff is likely quarantined. And we simply can't risk sending in an Agency strike team. With all our security breaches of late and the threat from Medlock and perhaps others inside our own organization, we cannot put this on record as an official Agency mission. We need someone who will not raise the suspicions of a potential traitor who may or may not already be inside the base. Also, we need someone who can fit into the small air shafts that lead into the emergency entry point. Lastly, and perhaps most important, we need someone who can approach a public tourist attraction without raising the suspicion of anyone who might be watching."

Everything that Director Isadoris had just said shocked and terrified me. But even so, one thing stuck out in particular.

"Did you just say 'public tourist attraction'?"

"That's right," Director Isadoris said, placing his palms flat on the desk in front of him. "The secret Agency base is located inside Mount Rushmore."

0101010101010100001010010101010010101010
10101000010010100101010010101010101010
90001⟨ ⟩0011001010101010101010101
901⟨ ⟩0010101010010101010100
101 CHAPTER 7 1010100101010101010
90⟨ ⟩11001010101010101010

THE DIRTY RAT WHO
SAVED THE WORLD

"**M**OUNT RUSHMORE?" I SAID. "YOU MEAN JUST LIKE IN THAT movie *Team America*?"

"We'd prefer not to discuss that, if you don't mind," said the director. "It's made things uncomfortable enough for us as it is."

Mount Rushmore. I could hardly believe it. There was a secret government laboratory hidden behind the faces of George Washington, Thomas Jefferson, Theodore Roosevelt, and Abraham Lincoln. A monument millions of people visited every summer. That our school, and probably dozens of others, took a trip to every school year.

And that's when it hit me. The Mount Rushmore field trip was departing on Friday morning.

"I get it," I said. "You want me to do it this weekend."

"Yes," replied Director Isadoris.

"But . . . Mr. Jensen, er, Agent Blue is one of the chaperones on the field trip. He has a believable reason to be there. Couldn't he handle this mission?"

"That's exactly the problem," Agent Blue interjected, speaking for the first time. "I'm one of three chaperones. I couldn't leave my post for any significant amount of time without drawing unwanted attention. Tourists and visitors are generally not allowed to get very close to the monument. There's a trail that ends well short of where an agent would need to be in order to infiltrate the base."

"You, however, will be just one of many students on the field trip," Director Isadoris added. "You can leave without attracting nearly as much attention, and even if you are caught, it will be interpreted as nothing more than a troublemaker causing trouble. An adult doing the same would appear much more unusual and suspicious."

"But I'm not even going on the field trip this weekend," I said. "I didn't earn it."

"We can take care of that," Agent Blue said.

I shook my head and gave him a grim smile. "Mr. Jensen, I don't mean to tell you you're wrong, but there's no way in the world Gomez will ever sign off on letting me come with. You know him as well as I do. How could you possibly make that happen?"

He glanced at Director Isadoris, who reached inside a desk drawer. I actually thought he was going to remove a high-tech mind-control device or something like that. But instead, he took out a red Tootsie Pop sucker. It looked ridiculously small in his frying pan hand. With a delicacy I'd have expected from a watch repair specialist or a heart surgeon, he deftly unwrapped it with his sausage fingers and then lodged it inside his right cheek. He did not offer either Agent Blue or me any candy. Not that I really wanted any just then.

Finally, he spoke.

"My grandpa used to tell my brothers and me a story when we went camping near Duluth every year. That's in Minnesota. You ever been there?"

I shook my head.

"That's too bad. It's nice. Or it was back then, who knows anymore. The story was about a man who lived north of the city, closer to the Minnesota Boundary

Waters, deep inside the forest. He lived off the land, fished for food, trapped animals, cut down trees to build a cabin, et cetera. You ever been in the Boy Scouts?"

I shook my head again.

"That's too bad. Hardly anyone knows how to handle themselves in a survival situation these days. How to live off the land the way man used to. They don't teach you much of that on TV or in video games. Listening to that survival-reality-show guy, Grizzly Skillet, or whatever his name is, is more likely to get you killed even faster than if you knew nothing at all. Anyhow, this fellow that lived off the land, David was his name, was chopping down a tree one day to stock up before the depths of the Minnesota winter set in. There's a real art to chopping down a tree correctly, and David knew that. But this one day, this one particular tree didn't fall the way it was supposed to. Maybe it was the slope of the hill. Or maybe a shift in the wind. Or maybe David simply made a rare mistake. Or maybe it was just bad luck. It doesn't matter. The point is, the tree fell on top of him and pinned down his leg. David was trapped."

I nodded dumbly, wondering where this was going and how it could possibly relate to Principal Gomez and the current situation. But I didn't say anything. I got the sense that, even though he had a harmless-looking sucker in his mouth, challenging Director Isadoris would be akin to jabbing at a sleeping grizzly bear with an extremely short stick while wearing a shirt made out of salmon filets.

"David knew that nobody would be coming for him. He lived ten miles north of the nearest paved road." Director Isadoris paused again to crunch down on the Tootsie Pop. "There was only one thing he could do. He just needed time to build up the courage."

"Oh, no . . . ," I said.

"Oh, yes," Director Isadoris said humorlessly. "He chopped off his own leg below the knee in order to free himself. He was willing to do what was necessary, no matter how scared he was. He was willing to make a sacrifice."

I hesitated. I thought I understood what he meant, but was afraid to venture a guess in case I was wrong.

"You'll have to make a sacrifice, too, Agent Zero," he said. "To get something, you have to give something. It's the natural order of things."

I swallowed as he stopped to chew on the Tootsie Roll in the center of his sucker. He attacked it with surprising ferocity given how calmly he'd worked down the candy part. When he finished, he glanced at Agent Blue, who continued.

"Carson, I've already spoken to Mr. Gomez, and he will let you go on the trip on three conditions."

I nodded, even though I wanted to stop him right there.

"First, you have to spend your lunch period tomorrow helping him continue to clean and repair his office. I've been told there was quite a bit of water damage, presumably from melted snow."

"Okay," I said. That didn't sound so bad. Not that the idea of spending an hour alone with Gomez sounded particularly fun, but it would be easy enough to get through. Like going to the dentist.

"Second," Agent Blue continued, "he insists that you understand that one more disciplinary incident of any kind between now and eighth-grade graduation will result in your immediate expulsion."

I nodded again. This condition was more serious, but if that's what it would take to complete my mission, I could agree. It's not as if I would be running another prank anytime soon. Besides, I'd kind of already reached the conclusion that pranks weren't really worth it anymore. They'd started to feel a little childish, actually.

"Finally," Agent Blue said, "you must give up the identities of all your accomplices in your most recent prank."

That hit me hard, like a Bonecrusher piledriver. Ratting out my best friends was worse than losing a leg. They trusted me.

"I can't," I said. "There has to be another way."

"I'm afraid there isn't," Agent Blue said. "Mr. Gomez was quite clear."

"I know it's a difficult pill to swallow," Isadoris said, sounding like a normal guy for the first time that afternoon. "But you're our last, best chance, Agent Zero. The only alternative would simply be to destroy the base. We can't risk the release of the bio weapon. Agent Nineteen's life, and the lives of all the agents and lab technicians at the base, depend on you. It's time to decide what you're willing to sacrifice to save them."

"But half the kids who helped me are going on the trip. If I rat them out, then they won't get to go," I said. "I mean, couldn't that affect the mission?"

"We've considered this possibility, yes," Agent Blue said, likely knowing perfectly well that Dillon and Danielle usually helped me with my pranks.

"Their inclusion on the trip isn't important," Director Isadoris said. "Yours is, Agent Zero. You're the one student we *need* on that trip. You're the one who can save Agent Nineteen, not your friends."

0000101010101010101001100101010101010101
0101010101010000101000101010010101010100
1010100001001010010101010010101010101010
00001   001100101010101010101010
001   00101010100101010100
       CHAPTER 8   10101001010101010101
101   1100101010101010101001

THE CHANDLERGAST

I WALKED ALONE BACK UP TOWARD THE SCHOOL FOR SIXTH period. And it was probably for the best. My mind was racing so much that I wouldn't have been able to focus long enough to even hear anybody talking to me, let alone make any sort of comprehensible conversation.

My new watch read: *69:54:13*.

Director Isadoris had given it to me before I'd left his office. It was a countdown clock set to the presumed time that the virus would kill everyone who had been exposed to it—including Agent Nineteen. They couldn't be sure of the precise time when those inside were exposed, but the watches would help to keep us on task. Even if the whole thing was a bit morbid. And manipulative. Looking down at it now, it seemed like they just wanted me to have a constant reminder of what was at stake so I wouldn't go back on ratting out my friends to Mr. Gomez.

Would I be able to do it, though? Rat out my trusting friends to Principal Gomez? Keeping secrets from my best friends had been hard enough. I didn't like secrets to begin with. But now I had to stab them in the back on top of adding even more layers of lies to the secrets I'd already been hiding from them.

I kicked at what looked like a stone in the snow. But it wasn't a stone. It was a small piece of a much larger chunk of dislodged pavement. My little toe exploded with pain as I stumbled and crashed face-first into a snow bank in the school parking lot.

After getting back up and wiping the dirty snow off my face, I decided that I had to tell Dillon and Danielle the truth. Not about the Agency and being a spy; witnessing what Medlock's breach had caused at Agency HQ had been enough of a warning about the perils of breaking your cover as an agent, even if it was to the two people you probably trusted more than anybody else in the world. But I had to tell them about Gomez, about giving up that they were my accomplices. The problem was, I had no idea how I was going to explain to them why I needed to do this.

By the time I met up with them after school, I still didn't have any answers.

"So where did you really go at lunch?" Dillon asked as I joined them outside the door where their mom picked them up every day.

"The bathroom," I said, patting my stomach. "That corned beef must have really jammed up my internal gears."

Dillon shook his head. "You're lying."

"No—" I started, but he cut me off.

"Don't even try to deny it, dude. I checked every single bathroom in the school. Even the teachers' lounge bathroom. You weren't in any of them."

"Gross!" Danielle said, smacking her twin brother's arm. "You looked under the stalls in every bathroom?"

"Hey, exposing conspiracies is dirty work sometimes," he said with a shrug, never taking his accusing eyes off me. "Plus, Andrew, from Carson's fifth period, said that he wasn't in class today. So where were you, for real?"

"Okay, okay, I didn't have to go to the bathroom," I admitted.

"I knew it!" Dillon said.

"But I can't tell you where I really was," I said. "At least, not here. Let's wait until we get to your house."

Dillon's face lit up like a psychedelic laser light show, complete with live heavy metal music. Nothing got him more excited than cryptic secrets that could only be talked about behind closed doors. Especially ones that revolved around him catching other people in lies.

Danielle, though, was genuinely concerned. "What's going on?" she asked. "Is everything okay?"

"I'll tell you soon," I said, pointing to their mom's car, which was just pulling up to the curb.

The ride to their place was unusually quiet. And tense. For me, at least. Danielle looked mostly nervous, and Dillon was so excited he was bouncing around like a dog on the way to the park. I honestly think that had his mom rolled down the window, he'd have stuck his head outside and slobbered all over the side of the car.

When we got to their house, we took off our winter coats and went downstairs to Dillon's room. His walls were lined with tinfoil the way other kids' walls were lined with movie, sports, and band posters. He claimed it helped scramble the Signal. Don't even get me started on what the Signal is.

"So what's the big secret?" Dillon asked, his eyes practically spinning in his skull.

Danielle closed the bedroom door and then joined us near Dillon's desk.

"Look, it's bad news, so don't get too excited," I said, forgetting that, for Dillon, there was no such thing as a good or bad secret. The only type of secret that existed was an exciting one.

"I knew it," Danielle said.

"It's really bad," I said. "I mean, like could-destroy-us-all bad."

"It's the Chandlergast, isn't it?" Dillon said, his smile finally fading.

"Not now," his sister groaned.

The Chandlergast was this creature that Dillon swore lived in the various parks around the town of Minnow. The creature roamed from park to park to stay hidden, feasting on dead squirrels and poor hapless homeless guys. According to Dillon, the Chandlergast was half dragon, half ostrich, and half caterpillar, and would eventually emerge from a cocoon having grown so large and powerful that it could wipe out the entire city. I once tried to point out to him that the creature couldn't have three halves, but he'd merely shrugged it off as a "technicality of phrasing and ultimately not that important given the potential devastation a full-grown Chandlergast would wreak."

"It's not the Chandlergast!" I said. "In fact, you know as well as I do that there's no such thing . . . Ah, never mind. Anyway, at lunch I was . . ."

I didn't get to finish my sentence because their doorbell interrupted me.

"That must be Jake!" Dillon said. "I invited him over today."

"Why?" Danielle asked, rolling her eyes.

"To strategize how we're going to get a photograph of Smallfoot in the Black Hills on our trip," Dillon said. "He *agrees* with me, unlike some of my friends, that we have at least a ten percent chance of a sighting."

"Don't you mean Bigfoot?" I said.

"Of course not, everybody knows Bigfoot isn't real," Dillon said with a dismissive scoff. "I mean, imagine an animal with feet that huge, it'd never be able to walk! Anyway, what's the problem with me inviting Jake over, Danielle?"

"There's no problem," she said. "I just . . . I thought he

was only helping us out for Prankpocalypse."

"Well, he was, but he turned out to be a pretty cool guy. Carson, you don't mind that he's here, do you?"

"No, it's fine," I said, glancing warily at Danielle. She was twirling a piece of her hair and not looking at either of us. "Actually, you might as well bring him downstairs. This involves him, too."

A minute later, we were all in the basement. Dillon told Jake that I was about to "reveal some crazy secret that would change the course of the world forever."

"Well, let's not go that far," I said. "Look, today at lunch I had to meet with Gomez in his office."

"What? Why?" Danielle asked, looking justifiably sick. "Prankpocalypse was a week ago, he never takes this long to punish you."

"Oh, man . . . ," Jake said, looking like he already knew where this was headed.

"Well, as per usual, he knows that I was behind Prankpocalypse," I said. "Except this time he actually has enough proof to expel me."

I watched their faces fall, and I don't think I'd ever felt so terrible in my life. Here I was, lying to my friends again.

"Oh, no! Carson!" Danielle said.

"I told you guys he had secret video cameras in his office," Dillon said quietly. "I've been saying it all year."

"Gomez is full of crap," Jake said confidently. "If he had anything on you, you'd already be gone."

"That's the problem," I said. "He's holding out because he wants me to give him the names of all my accomplices. If I give everyone up, then he promised that none of us would be expelled. But it would mean no Rushmore trip for the kids I turn in, and a ton of detention besides that."

Danielle looked as if she was about to cry. Dillon, for once, was also speechless. He just sat there and stared at me in shock. No crazy theories, no insane stories or hypotheticals over what could have caused our predicament. Jake looked completely zoned out, perhaps lost in thought. Or maybe he was legitimately in shock, like people sometimes are in movies after they barely escape a horrible accident.

"I know," I said after a few moments. "It's bad. I don't know what to do."

"Turn us in," Danielle said softly. "You have to. You can't let yourself be expelled. Besides, nobody forced us to help you. We all knew the risks."

"But the trip . . . I know how much you've been looking forward to it."

It was true. Danielle especially had been looking forward to her chance to get to go on the seventh-grade Mount Rushmore field trip since she was eight years old and first found out about it. She loved vacations, camping, history, science, and school. This trip was one of the few times in life that all five of those things got combined into one awesome weekend. And now it was about to get ruined. She looked as devastated as I felt for her. It was almost enough for me to just tell them the complete truth, so they'd know what was really at stake and why I wasn't going to bite the bullet for them like I always promised I would if we ever got caught.

"When do you need to tell him by?" Dillon asked.

"Tomorrow at lunch."

"Ah, crud," he said.

And that pretty much summed up the whole situation. The four of us looked at our feet and the wall and one another with expressions of utter defeat on our faces. That's when Jake's face lit up.

"Guys, this isn't as bad as it seems," he said. "Carson, just tell Gomez I was your only helper."

"What?" I said.

"No way, man, you don't have to take the fall for us," Dillon added.

"Trust me," Jake said. "My mom is on the school board, remember? And she practically pays for the whole trip every year. Gomez might stick me with a bit of detention, but there's no way he'll kick me off the trip and risk upsetting my mom."

We all looked at one another for a few moments. I figured Dillon and Danielle were both debating the same thing that I was: Could that be true? Was Jake really above the law on this? And if so, what good reason would there be to not let him take the fall?

"You're sure?" I asked finally.

Jake nodded. "I can handle some detention. I've never had it before, and I've always been curious what it's like anyway."

None of us knew what to say. Even Danielle was looking at Jake with a newfound respect.

"Don't worry about it, guys," Jake said, laughing. "It's nice that having my mom on the school board will actually come in handy for once. Now, I think Dillon and I have some Smallfoot strategies to discuss, right?"

Dillon grinned and Danielle groaned. She never bought in to Dillon's theories, but as the two of them sat down to look at articles on Jake's tablet, I thought I could see the smallest hint of jealousy on her face.

CHAPTER 9

EATING FISH HEADS
UNDER A BRIDGE

SPENDING LUNCH PERIOD WITH PRINCIPAL GOMEZ ALONE IN his office the next day was about as fun as it sounded. Which is to say, I'd rather have spent the hour eating raw fish heads under the Seventh Street bridge. He spent the first ten minutes gloating about how I wasn't nearly as smart as I thought I was, and how he knew he'd get me eventually. At one point he even admitted that he was happy I was getting to go on the trip because then it'd be one less day I could cause trouble at his school. And all that is not even mentioning the actual work of cleaning up the mess.

As I tried to help him copy the water-damaged documents from the bottom drawer of his desk, I couldn't help but think that Prankpocalypse didn't really seem all that funny anymore. I even almost started to feel a little bad about what we did to Gomez. But his sour mood that afternoon helped me get over the guilt pretty quickly.

"I just don't understand why Mr. Jensen consistently argues on your behalf," he groused as he transcribed one of the documents onto a new sheet of paper. "All I see is an entitled, spoiled troublemaker who's headed for a lifetime of disappointment when he realizes that there won't always be someone around to bail him out for his myriad of mistakes."

I thought that was a little unfair, but I held my tongue, even resisting the urge to point out that if he would just enter all these documents into his computer as opposed to transcribing them by hand, he'd never run into this problem again. It seemed like he should have been smart enough to figure that out on his own, having risen to the position of school principal and all.

"And for the life of me, I just can't figure out why on earth they want you to come with them on the Mount Rushmore trip," he continued ranting. "With you out there in the wild, they'll be lucky to get even half of the kids back alive."

"Mr. Gomez, I have no idea what you're talking about," I said, truly surprised that he would actually say these kinds of things to a student.

"Don't play dumb with me," he said. "You've earned every bit of your reputation."

I didn't say anything else, but instead kept digging through the mess of crusted file folders filled with crinkled, ink-smeared papers.

We worked in silence for the rest of the lunch period. At the end, Mr. Gomez made a big show of digging around for a few sheets of paper that were lying right on top in his briefcase. He plopped them down on his desk.

"Are you ready to put an end to your foolishness?" he asked.

"Um, sure," I said.

"This is what we call a Disciplinary Plan of Corrective Action Contract, or a DPCAC," Mr. Gomez said, sliding the papers across the desk toward me.

For some reason, this reminded me of my very first meeting in Agent Nineteen's secret office, the one where they told me the truth about the Agency. Or as much of the truth as they were allowed to reveal, which likely hadn't been much. That meeting had been filled with mysterious acronyms and documents as well.

Gomez continued, "It states that in exchange for allowing you to go on the school's field trip to Mount Rushmore, you agree to the following: One, you will provide the names of all accomplices or participants in your most recent act of vandalism against our school. Two, you hereby agree that one more disciplinary action against you for the remainder of your time here through the end of next school year may, and likely will, result in your immediate expulsion. Understand?"

I nodded.

"Even something as simple as chewing gum in class can get you expelled now, you understand?" Gomez seemed to relish driving the point home.

"Yeah, I got it," I said.

"Good," he said, not even trying to hide his grin now. "Then please write down the names of all your accomplices right here. And if I find out that you left off a single name, that'll be it for you, Carson. Get me?"

I nodded and grabbed the pen he was holding out toward me. I pulled the form closer and scribbled down Jake's name, and then put down the pen.

"That's it?" he asked.

"Yup, just the two of us," I said, marveling at how much easier it was to lie to Gomez than it was to my friends.

"That seems unlikely, given the extent of the damage," he said.

"Well, we got here early and worked all night," I said.

"Very well then," Gomez said, nodding. "You can sign and date the last page."

I did as I was instructed. Then I set down the pen again and slid the contract back across the desk. I waited while he flipped through it and scanned the pages. He said nothing.

"Uh, can I go now?" I said. "Fifth period starts soon and I need to go to my locker."

He looked up at me, seeming surprised that I was still there.

"Yes, you may go," he said. "I'll let Mr. Jensen and Ms. Pearson know that you have my approval to go on the field trip tomorrow. One of them will call your parents this evening to discuss the details."

"Okay, well, uh, thanks, Mr. Gomez," I said.

He didn't say anything, so I turned and headed for the exit.

"One last thing," Gomez said as I got to the door. I

looked back, being careful not to give him any reason to cancel the contract. "Let this be a valuable lesson to you, Carson. That *all* your actions eventually do have consequences."

10101010101010100110010101010101010101010
0101010101010000101001010100101010100
1010100001001010010101010010101010101010
00001   00110010101010101010101010
010   0101010100101010100
101   10101001010101010101010
00   1001010101010101010

CHAPTER 10

THE WORLD ENDS IN 2029

"**H**OW DID IT GO WITH GOMEZ?" DILLON ASKED WHEN I walked into sixth-period life sciences that day.

"Yeah, man, how did he take it?" Jake asked, his leg bouncing under his desk like he'd just spent the last three hours chugging a giant cooler of Gatorade.

The three of us sat right next to one another for sixth period. Which was normally pretty awesome. In school, each class is only as bearable as your proximity to friends.

"It went okay," I said. "He bought it."

Jake nodded.

"You're still okay?" I asked.

"I'm fine," he said. "My mom's always so busy drinking cocktails and gossiping with the other rich ladies at the country club that she probably won't even notice whatever detention they give me anyway."

I nodded. Man, if I were the one taking the fall for something like this, I'd never be this cool about it.

"So when do your detentions start then?" Dillon asked.

"Not sure," I said. "Whenever I get back, I guess."

"Get back from where?" Dillon asked.

I'd completely forgotten that he didn't know about the me-getting-to-go-on-the-trip part of the deal. Obviously he was going to find out tomorrow either way, but I couldn't think of a reason to explain that part away.

"Oh, we're just going to my aunt and uncle's house over in Willisville this weekend," I said. Man, keeping secrets was complicated. It created a constantly growing web of interconnected lies that were almost impossible to keep intact. It was more stressful than anything else I'd ever had to do in my life, including guarding a ticking time bomb for two days earlier that year when I'd first gotten myself mixed up in this whole secret-agent thing.

"Please stop talking, boys, the bell rang thirty seconds

ago," said Ms. Greenwood from the front of the class.

"Sorry," Jake said, waving at her.

Halfway through class, a note plopped onto my desk. I looked back at Dillon. He nodded for me to open it, frowning in that way that he did whenever he talked about this one theory he had about how the world was going to run out of oil by the year 2029, something he called Peak Oil, and how it would descend into a postapocalyptic wasteland like in *Mad Max*. Then I'd ask him who was Mad Max. And he'd always reply, *You'll find out in 2029.*

I opened the note:

I'm so sorry. I can't believe you got caught.

I wrote back:

It's okay. At least you guys are still going to Rushmore!

I tossed the note back to him when the teacher wasn't looking. Then I buried my head in my arms and tried not to think about Agent Nineteen's impending death or how I was going to explain to my friends that I was going on the school trip the day after I got busted for the biggest prank in school history. Constantly lying to your best friends was something my agency training never covered.

CHAPTER 11

THE WAL-MART CONNECTION

JUST AFTER DINNER THAT NIGHT, THE PHONE RANG. ABOUT twenty minutes later, my mom came downstairs and knocked on my bedroom door. She came into my room with a huge grin on her face.

"Guess who just called?" she asked, and then kept talking before even letting me get a guess in. "Mr. Jensen from school. Turns out they had a student get sick and drop out of the Mount Rushmore field trip. And you'll never guess whose name came up to replace him."

"Uh, me?" I said. "Being that you're in here asking me these questions?"

She laughed. "How exciting is that, Carson?"

I nodded and tried to pretend that I was excited to go on a simple, fun, carefree school field trip with my friends and that it wasn't actually all just a setup for me to go on some insane mission that involved secret bases and deadly viruses.

"Come on, put on your shoes," she said.

"Why?"

"The bus leaves tomorrow morning at seven! We have to go to Wal-Mart to get you some supplies! Then we have to get you packed!"

I hadn't seen my mom this giddy in forever. She was always a happy-enough person, I guess, but this was on a whole other level. It was likely because she was used to having two sons who had turned getting detention into an Olympic event. Turns out, she preferred having kids who get to go on special field trips usually reserved for the "good kids." Who knew?

At Wal-Mart, we were in the outdoors section picking out a flashlight when we ran into Jake.

"Hey, Carson, what are you doing here?" he asked.

"Shopping, of course."

"Going camping?" he asked, looking at the cart full of camping gear.

I noticed that his mom was nowhere in sight. Did he just come here to hang out or something? It wouldn't be unheard of. In a town this small, sometimes people go to Wal-Mart to bum around. Yes, seriously.

"Yeah, turns out I get to go on the Rushmore trip," I said.

"What?" he practically shouted. "How did you pull that off?"

I stepped on his toes as subtly as I could to shut him up.

"My mom, dude," I whispered, motioning toward my mom, who was just a few feet away, reading the back of a flashlight package.

"Oh, right, sorry!"

"Anyway," I said, ready to try out the story I'd come up with, "Gomez apparently said something to Mr. Jensen about how our new agreement should mean a new start for me or something like that. So I guess he's letting me go on this trip to test my commitment. I don't know. I really think he was probably just looking for a way to get rid of me for an extra day."

Jake nodded. "Cool. Man, Dillon and Danielle are going to be so excited."

"I know, but I want to surprise them tomorrow morning on the bus so don't text them tonight or anything, okay?"

He grinned and nodded.

"Sure thing. Do you think you'll get to tent with Dillon and me?"

I shrugged. "I kind of just found out about this. Apparently some other kid dropped out."

"Oh, weird," Jake said. "Well, his loss is our gain!"

"Yeah," I said, glancing back at my mom. She was looking at blowtorches now. What kind of trip did she think this was?

"Your mom seems pretty cool," Jake said. He was watching her also.

"What do you mean?"

"You know, bringing you here all excited to buy you supplies and stuff. My mom just gave me her credit card and told me to come here and get whatever I wanted."

"Yeah, she's all right, I guess." I can't say I ever really thought about it. I figured moms generally lived for stuff like buying you supplies for school trips. "Well, I better get back to shopping, but I guess I'll see you tomorrow."

"Yeah, see you then," Jake said as he turned and wandered off in the direction of the toy section.

CHAPTER 12

REPLICA FACES ARE
ALL THE RAGE

MY MOM WAS STILL ACTING LIKE A GIDDY NUTCASE WHEN SHE dropped me off in the school parking lot the morning of the trip with a new duffel bag full of clothes, a new sleeping bag, and a backpack full of "supplies."

"Have fun!" She gave me a hug.

"Okay, Mom," I said.

"Don't get into trouble. Take lots of pictures. Call me every day!"

"Okay, Mom," I said again, trying not to sound annoyed.

"I'll see you when you get home."

My stomach started to hurt as I realized that I might not be coming home at all, depending on what I found inside the secret government base that I was going to infiltrate tomorrow afternoon. I hadn't considered what my mom would do if something went wrong. I'd never seen her cry before. The thought alone almost made me start crying.

"Love you," she said with a final squeeze.

"Yeah, love you, too," I said, feeling even worse.

Mr. Jensen, aka Agent Blue, was waiting by the bus's lower luggage compartment. He nodded at me as I approached.

"Good to see you, Carson," he said.

I nodded back at him as he took my sleeping bag and duffel bag. He tossed them deep into the bus storage compartment.

"You're the first one here, so you get your pick of seats," he said, motioning toward the bus door.

The bus itself wasn't a normal school bus. It wasn't yellow and didn't have seats that were basically rows of wooden benches covered with a thin layer of fake leather. This bus was huge, with tinted windows, and it had padded seats with headrests. There was also a small bathroom in the rear.

As I made my way toward the back, I noticed a small slip of paper in my coat pocket. I pulled it out. There was a message scrawled on it in the tiniest printed handwriting I'd ever seen.

Meet me behind the charter bus tonight at 11 p.m. for mission briefing. Ingest this message.

Agent Blue must have slipped it into my pocket when I was giving him my luggage. Once again, I thought about my mom driving to work, unaware of what I was about to do, and my body felt completely empty.

After eating the small piece of paper, I took a seat and checked my watch. Agent Nineteen had approximately thirty hours left to live. I sighed and watched out the window for my friends. Jake showed up first. He smiled and waved at me when he boarded the bus. I moved over so he could sit down.

"You ever been to Rushmore before?" he asked.

"No, have you?"

He shook his head. "My parents used to go all the time when they were younger, though. Before they got bogged down by cement shoes. That's what my mom calls my brother and me: cement shoes. She always says she can't wait for us to go to college so she and Dad can get their life back. Whatever that means."

"Uh . . . okay," I said, not sure if he was joking around with me or not. It sounded like he had a pretty weird family. I'd known Jake for a while, but we'd never been actual friends until his old best friend, Anders, moved away last month, and then he just kind of melted into our group. We were happy to welcome him. He always seemed like a strange kid, but that's what I liked about him. North Dakota was too boring as it was to hang out with ordinary people on top of that.

"Anyway, they said I'll love it, that it's right up my alley."

"Are you a presidents buff or something?" I asked.

"No, not really. I've just always loved faces. Like, replica faces. Paintings, drawings, masks, sculptures, you know."

I nodded, even though I didn't really know at all. Replica faces seemed like a strange thing to be into. But then again, my best friend thought that Pizza Hut had some secret operation in place to domesticate pelicans by the year 2035, so who was I to judge?

"There's this guy, Chuck Close, who paints these amazing portraits," Jake continued. "These massive paintings of faces. He's my favorite artist in the world. I might pee my pants when I finally see Rushmore, I'll be so excited. Have you ever done that? Peed your pants out of excitement?"

I thought back to a few months ago when I'd peed my pants in class on purpose to avoid getting caught with Betsy—the secret, self-destructing data device I'd accidentally activated. I figured that could kind of be attributed to excitement. Then again, I wasn't sure if Jake was even being serious.

"Uh . . . maybe?" I said.

Jake laughed and nodded. Then he looked out the window and grinned. "Dillon and Danielle are here!" he said.

Their car was just pulling into the parking lot. Several moments later there was a gasp as Danielle spotted us from the front of the bus. She practically sprinted to the back.

"What the heck are you doing here?" she asked, sitting down in front of Jake and me.

Dillon sat next to her, grinning.

"I knew it!" he said.

"You did not," Danielle said, but she was smiling, too.

"I did! I've been saying all week that something was up with this trip!"

"What you said all week," Danielle replied, raising her fingers up like quotation marks, "is that this trip was really a secret mission to break into the hidden vault behind Lincoln's nose, where thousands of gold bars are kept. Then you said that was the origin of the phrase 'digging for gold,' used with respect to nose picking. Then later this week you claimed that the trip was part of a secret experiment to see what happened when thirty middle school kids get trapped inside a bus with a family of hungry black bears—a theory that I personally didn't find very funny. Then, after that . . ."

"Okay, okay!" Dillon finally stopped her. "Maybe I didn't predict that Carson would be coming with. But my theory about the gold bars still stands."

"Whatever," Danielle said. "The real question is, Carson, how did you manage to get yourself on this trip?"

I proceeded to tell them the same story I'd told Jake the night before at Wal-Mart. They seemed to buy it.

Meanwhile, I was now lying to my best friends often enough to feel like a professional liar. A real snake. And the worst part was, the more I lied, the better I seemed to do it.

CHAPTER 13

THE CARD SHARK

A LOT OF PEOPLE WHO AREN'T FROM NORTH DAKOTA NEVER seem to understand just how big the state is. They think that you can just drive from one end to the other in an hour. Well, they're wrong. North and South Dakota are both huge. It takes over five hours just to drive across one of them. If you're lucky. Because most of the time the interstates and highways are completely torn apart by road construction due to the harsh, karate-kick-to-your-face winters being so completely devastating to pavement.

Likewise, driving from Minnow, North Dakota, to Mount Rushmore National Memorial in South Dakota was no trip around the block. It was a ten-hour trek through the flat, boring wastelands of the upper prairie. In fact, we weren't even going to make it there in time to see Mount Rushmore that same day. The plan was to get to the Black Hills area Friday evening and then camp out somewhere near the monument. Then we'd head up to see it on Saturday morning. Which was also when I'd have to embark on my dangerous solo mission. At which point Agent Nineteen would have just a few hours left to live.

At that moment, though, we were still on the road, and when you're in a charter bus with your best friends, a long ride really doesn't feel so long. Especially if you can get a poker game going in the back.

"You guys ever play Texas Hold 'Em?" Jake asked once we all realized our smart phone and handheld gaming system batteries would never last the entire drive.

We played poker using our snack and souvenir money, keeping the antes pretty low so nobody had to go without snacks for the rest of the trip. But with seven of us in, there was still a chance to win a decent amount of extra cash.

After an hour or so, I was down almost five bucks. I'm usually not such a bad poker player, but the fact that the mission was drawing closer with every mile had me more than a little distracted. And people were starting to notice. I needed to get my head back in the game, if only to keep from blowing my cover.

That's when Danielle dealt me *the* hand. A pair of aces. The best hand you can get in Texas Hold 'Em. This was my chance.

I played it cool and didn't bet anything right away. If you bet too much, people will fold and then you won't win anything, even with the best hand. Three people stayed in: Jake, Danielle, and this one kid named Carl, who nobody really wanted to let play because he smells like moldy Greek yogurt apparently due to some medical condition he has. But then again, we're not bullies, so of course we let him play.

Dillon folded, like he did almost every hand. He was terrible at poker, since, you know, he always assumed that every other player was trying to cheat in some outrageously complicated manner. But when you fold every time and the ante is only a nickel, you won't end up losing much money.

Anyway, there were four of us in for the flop, which

included two low clubs and the ace of spades. That meant I now had three aces. Poker pros call it a set. Don't ask me why.

I tried not to let how excited I was show. It was a virtual lock that I'd win the hand. I just had to keep everyone else from folding too soon.

"Ace of spades?" Dillon said. "Oh, man, it's a Dark Grave Digger. You all know what that means . . ."

The group groaned. There were certain card combinations that Dillon was apparently convinced spelled out certain cosmic paths for those playing the game. It had been funny for the first hour, but now it was starting to bum us all out, since almost all of Dillon's combinations led to some sort of gory and inescapable death.

"This bus is going to drive off a cliff and burst into flames when the full moon draws to its highest point," Dillon said.

"This is South Dakota—there aren't many cliffs around here," Danielle said.

"Actually, the Black Hills has several cliffs," Carl said. "However, the current phase of the moon is three-fourths waning, so we'll be fine either way."

Dillon breathed a sigh of relief, and we all burst out laughing. I looked at my cards again. That had actually just been the perfect distraction to make everyone forget the pure glee that had probably flashed in my eyes when I saw that ace flop.

I checked, which means I didn't bet anything this time around. I was waiting for some poor fish to make the first move.

Everyone else checked as well, and I hid my disappointment. The turn card was a jack of hearts. Checks all around again. Now I was sure nobody had anything good, which meant I needed to hope someone got a decent-enough hand to make a bet.

The river card was the eight of spades. I checked again, hoping someone would bet to try to buy the pot.

Danielle also checked.

So did Carl.

Jake took the bait and bet seventy-five cents. A pretty bold bet considering the biggest pot so far had been about two dollars. He thought nobody had a good hand, and so we'd all fold to his big bet and he'd take the antes. That was precisely what I wanted him to think.

"Raise two fifty," I said, throwing down the money.

Jake raised an eyebrow, but I knew he was more surprised than he let on. That was the payoff for the old check-raise maneuver. My hand twitched, waiting for him to fold, waiting to reach out and pull all that delicious cash back toward me.

But he didn't fold.

"Five dollars," Jake said calmly.

Gasps followed his reraise. Then everyone's eyes turned toward me as the bus jumbled across a rough patch of the highway. I looked down at my two aces and then back at the table where the other five cards sat, faceup.

I examined Jake's face. He stared back at me without blinking. It was almost like he was inviting me to try to read him, to figure out what he had. Like he had nothing at all to hide.

"What are you gonna do now, Carson?" he taunted in a friendly way.

I looked at the cards again. What did he have? Best I could guess, he had two pair. Perhaps he was holding the last ace in the deck, and was convinced his pair of aces and another pair would be enough to win the pot. But he was wrong.

"Call," I said.

"Let's see them," Danielle said.

I flipped over my aces. "Sorry, man."

"No, I'm sorry," Jake said, flipping over two spades.

"A flush. Or a troupe of Dark Grave Diggers, as Dillon might say."

"A flush?" I said. "But that's only four spades."

Danielle spoke up, too. "Carson's right. The ace, the eight on the river, and the two in your hand make four, dude," she said.

Jake blinked. "Look again."

We all looked down at the cards. The first one that Danielle dealt was a spade. I could have sworn it had been a club. How distracted was I?

"That's not right!" Danielle insisted. "I dealt a club. I know it." She looked around the table, as if the first club had gotten up and ran away or something.

"I don't know what to tell you guys," Jake said, gathering the money. "Except it looks like I'm going to be swimming in snacks tomorrow."

I sat there dumbfounded. The flush was the only possible hand that could have beaten mine. He'd sharked me, plain and simple. In that moment I knew that he'd known since that last card turned over that he had me beat. He let me think he was playing into my hand, when in reality I was only playing right into his. And here I thought *I* was a good liar.

Dillon gave Jake a high five while Danielle stared at

Jake suspiciously. I appreciated her being on my side, but it didn't really matter. It was my own stupid fault for being too distracted to see the card right when it was dealt. I checked my watch. We'd been on the road for six hours, a little more than halfway to where we'd camp that night.

"Whose deal is it?" I asked, but my voice was hollow. Not because I had just lost the hand, but because I was back to thinking about the mission, now less than twenty-four hours away. Which meant Agent Nineteen potentially could be dead in less than a day. I could die, too, and my parents wouldn't even know why. People's lives were resting on my shoulders, their combined weight so heavy it felt like my back was going to crack in half. And there I was playing poker for quarters on a bus.

And right then, more than ever before, despite being crammed on a bus with thirty kids, three teachers, and a bus driver, I had never felt more alone in my whole life.

CHAPTER 14

THE FLAMMABLE TENT

WE GOT TO THE CAMPGROUND AROUND SIX THAT EVENING. The three school chaperones—Ms. Pearson, science teacher; Mr. Gist, history teacher; and Mr. Jensen, social studies teacher and secret agent—helped us unpack our supplies from the bus and carry them to our campsite. Then Mr. Gist started cooking us dinner over a fire pit in the center of our rented camping space while the other two helped us set up our tents.

At least, that's what we were supposed to have been doing. In reality, it was like a tornado of cheap canvas and plastic poles. Most of the eleven tents were lopsided and looked like some sort of spiny techno-monster from a bizarre anime film.

One poor group of kids managed to mess up so badly that their longest tent pole launched a backpack up into a nearby tree like a catapult. While Mr. Jensen climbed the tree to retrieve it, the other chaperone, Ms. Pearson, was busy helping two other groups try to find out why their tent door was facing the ground.

The chaos left Dillon, Jake, and me alone to set up our tent by ourselves. But really, how hard could it be? Just a few months ago I'd helped to save the world, and in about eighteen hours I'd be infiltrating a secret government base to save a bunch of real-life spies. But it turns out that foiling the complicated plans of a demented evil genius was a whole lot easier than building a tent that came with instructions. After just five minutes, we had a complete disaster on our hands. Our tent looked like it was more likely to randomly burst into flames during the night than it was to keep out bugs or rain.

"What did we do wrong?" Jake asked.

"It must be in the air here," Dillon said. "Can't you smell that?"

"Don't even say it," I warned him, but he was already

off on another one of his theories.

"There's, like, some toxic vapor in the air. I can feel it penetrating my brain and making me stupider by the second. Quick, ask me a simple math problem."

This is about where I would usually stop indulging him, but Jake wasn't as used to Dillon yet.

"What's ten plus fourteen times seven, divided by six?" Jake asked.

"I said simple!" Dillon shouted, clutching at his brain like it was about to explode.

I rolled my eyes and focused on freeing the poles from their incorrect places in the tent holes.

"What's seven plus nineteen?" Jake tried again.

"Oh, no!" Dillon yelled in a panic. "I don't know the answer! I'm getting dumber and dumber by the second. My brains are going to be pudding within minutes. Ahhh! Oh . . . wait, it's twenty-six. Never mind."

Jake laughed, but only because he thought Dillon was joking around. As for me, I was suddenly aware that Dillon might've actually been right about this one. We were just a few miles away from Mount Rushmore now, where a deadly airborne virus had been released. Maybe it had gotten out into the open through Teddy Roosevelt's nostrils? The most deadly presidential sneeze in history?

"Carson? Hello?" Jake was waving his hand in front of my face. "Dillon thinks he figured out what we did wrong with the tent."

I looked up and saw Dillon rolling around inside our mess of deflated tent and plastic poles. And right then, even with the threat of a deadly virus hanging over our heads, I couldn't help but laugh so hard that my side started aching.

CHAPTER 15

WHY NOBODY EVER
MESSES WITH AUSTRALIA

An hour after arriving at the campground, after finally managing to get the tents constructed, we were all sitting around the campfire in a circle. We ate a dinner that consisted of baked beans heated right in the can over the fire, corn on the cob, and ham sandwiches. It was pretty delicious, much better than I expected, especially since I didn't even think I was that hungry.

During dinner, the chaperones told us about what our expectations were over the next two days. We'd be learning all kinds of stuff: geology and history, mostly.

But there was a writing component, too. We had to keep journals of everything we saw and learned over the course of the trip.

Ms. Pearson talked about what we were supposed to write each day, but I wasn't really listening to her. I was thinking about Agent Nineteen. About what he might be doing or thinking at that very moment. Did he think he was going to die? Or did he assume that the Agency had some covert mission planned to save him and the rest of the lab workers? What would he think if he knew that mission was basically to just send in a seventh-grade goof-off? Would he go back to thinking he was doomed? This was all assuming he was even still alive. I suddenly felt like my baked beans were going to make a return trip up my esophagus.

But I also wondered if he felt lonely, trapped inside the base with the other dying agents. Because that's how I felt. I glanced over at Dillon and Danielle, taking notes on what Ms. Pearson was saying. I was hiding almost everything important happening to me from my friends, which made it feel like there was a steel air lock between us all the time.

After dinner, we helped the three teachers clean up and put away the dishes. Then they herded us back to our seats around the campfire. We sat in a huge semi-circle, leaving open the part of it where all the smoke was blowing.

"One of Mr. Jensen's favorite traditions on this trip is to tell campfire stories," Mr. Gist said. "We've done it every year since he and I started chaperoning this trip, and every year at least one student passes out from sheer terror."

Everyone laughed nervously, trying to figure out if he was kidding.

"And so I'll let Mr. Jensen start us off," he said.

Our eyes turned toward Mr. Jensen, who already had a flashlight shining under his chin, casting his face with creepy shadows. His grin was as cheesy as it was wicked. We all laughed. Mr. Jensen did, too. But then his face turned serious again.

"My tale takes place in a forest not unlike the one we're camping in now," he said, switching off the flashlight so we could actually focus on the story. "It involves a troop of scouts out on their annual canoe trip to the Minnesota Boundary Waters, where there are almost no roads and very few signs of civilization. They were in their third night of the trip, and so far everything was going as planned. There had been no canoe capsizes, no major injuries, they'd even managed to catch their own dinner in the river that day.

"That night, the two scoutmasters and twelve scouts made a campfire and sat around it roasting marshmallows and telling scary stories just like we are at this very moment. At midnight, just as the full moon reached its brightest and highest point, the scouts retreated to their tents while the scoutmasters cleaned up and put out the fire.

"An hour later, four scouts awoke to a rustling noise just outside their tent. They heard raspy, heavy breathing followed by the sound of something scraping across the ground. They suspected the other scouts were pulling a prank. And so they slowly unzipped their tent. The bravest of the four scouts poked his head outside. Suddenly his body convulsed as the other three heard a primal growl. The bravest kid fell back inside the tent. But it didn't take long for the other scouts to notice that his head was gone.

"They screamed in terror just as a large set of claws tore through the side of their tent. The three of them scrambled out into the night. The bright moon lit up the campsite just enough for them to see a large hulking beast rush past them and tear into another nearby tent.

"The beast had gray, matted fur and easily stood six feet tall, even hunched over slightly. It had long, curved, dark claws that looked as if they could slice a small car in half. Its jaws were packed with twisted, jagged teeth. It lunged inside the tent headfirst and pulled back a short time later with a poor scout clamped inside its mouth.

"One of the counselors stepped in between the three scouts and the beast. 'What are you still doing here? Run!' he screamed.

"The three scouts didn't wait for him to say it a second time as they turned and sprinted into the dark forest. They stayed together as they ran, eventually finding a massive tree to stop and rest behind. They panted, looking at one another's terrified expressions and finding little comfort in them.

"'Should we go back?' one of them eventually asked. The others seemed unsure of what to do. After a short debate, they all decided to slowly work their way back toward the camp to see if anyone else had survived. They weren't entirely sure if they were headed in the right direction, but before long they found themselves in a clearing. One of their scoutmasters was also there with his back to them, hunched over and shaking.

"'Mr. G?' one of the kids said cautiously as they

approached. 'Are you okay?'

"He didn't reply. Instead he merely kept shaking. And so the three scouts walked around to face him. Mr. G's eyes were wide and his lips quivered. They waited for him to say something. Anything. After a moment longer it seemed like he finally realized they were there. He reached out for them, and that's when he vomited. As the scouts watched, terrified, blood and guts poured out of his mouth, and, among them, the tattered remains of a scout merit badge. Then, he opened his mouth again and . . ."

"AAAAAIIIEEEEEEEEEE!" Mr. Gist let out a shrill, blood-curdling cry that startled us so badly that at least fifteen kids screamed and one fell backward off the log he'd been perched on.

Mr. Gist and Mr. Jensen laughed as we tried to recover. I had to admit, even my heart was racing. Once we'd all calmed down enough, we applauded. Well, those of us who weren't mad or embarrassed for being scared so badly.

Then Mr. Gist took the flashlight and told a story about how hard it would be for us all to find jobs after college in the future. I got the joke about how that was a "scary" story, but still didn't find it all that funny or scary.

Danielle, however, looked truly horrified.

Next, Ms. Pearson told a supposedly true story about aliens abducting three fishermen from this very area twenty years ago. The three men were missing for two days and then suddenly turned up near their campsite one morning without any memory of what had happened during the time they went missing. Supposedly, they all eventually recalled the same horrific alien abduction story while under psychiatric hypnosis. It was pretty freaky.

Then the teachers asked if any of the students had a horror story to share. A few kids told some lame ghost stories. Jake retold the plot of this zombie book he read called *The Infects*. It was a little scary since it took place out in the woods with a bunch of kids. But he lost some points, in my opinion, since it wasn't really his own story.

Dillon told a story about how we all had implants in our brains that the governor-general of Australia was using to control our thought patterns. Which is why nobody ever says anything bad about Australia. Most of the other kids laughed at his story, but I knew he'd really meant it to be scary and probably actually believed it was true.

"Well, on *that* note," Mr. Gist said after Dillon

finished, "we should get to bed."

"Lights out in fifteen minutes," Ms. Pearson said. "And remember, if you need to use the bathroom in the middle of the night, you must bring one of your tent partners with you."

The kids groaned.

"It's for your own safety," she said. "That's also why I recommend you all use the bathroom before you go to bed."

As we dispersed and Ms. Pearson and Mr. Gist put out the fire, I was already trying to figure out how to deal with this new challenge. I had to get out of my tent at eleven o'clock to meet Agent Blue for the mission briefing. How would I explain to Jake and Dillon where I was going, and keep them from following me? Could I sneak out once they'd fallen asleep? It seemed unlikely. No kid passes out before midnight on a Friday night camping trip with his best friends.

For the fortieth time this week, I had to remind myself that telling my friends about my double life as a secret agent was not an option. No matter how much easier it would be.

CHAPTER 16

MANBEARPIG

THAT NIGHT, FOR THE FIRST TIME IN WHAT FELT LIKE FOREVER, luck seemed to be on my side.

When we went back to our tents, I made a big deal about how late it was and pretended to fall asleep. My plan was to act really tired in the hopes that everyone else would want to go to sleep early, too. And the crazy thing was, it seemed to be working.

At 10:45, just as I was considering making my move to sneak out of the tent, I felt a hand on my shoulder.

"Carson." It was Jake, whispering.

"What? Huh?" I mumbled, pretending to wake up.

"I'm sorry, but I gotta go," he said. "I hope it's all right I woke you. You're closest to the tent door."

"Oh, yeah, right," I said, and started pulling on my shoes. I ran through the situation in my mind as I put on my coat. On one hand, this was pretty lucky, as I now had a believable reason to leave the tent right on time. On the other, I'd be escorting Jake to the bathroom and might not be able to shake him so I could go meet up with Agent Blue. But the solution became obvious as we walked toward the campground bathrooms that were about a hundred yards away from our group of tents.

"So . . . I might be a while," Jake said uncomfortably. "I have to, uh, go save the world."

"No problem," I said, trying to keep my nerves from making my voice shake. "It happens."

"Thanks for being so cool about it," he said. "You don't have to, like, stand in the bathroom with me. That'd be gross. I won't tell anyone if you want to hang outside the bathroom until I'm done."

I nodded. This couldn't have worked out any better.

As soon as he went inside the well-lit campground bathroom, I snuck away from the building and headed back toward where the charter bus was parked. The faint light from the tall lamps near the bathrooms lit up the path just enough for me to see where I was going without a flashlight, but that didn't keep it from being spooky. There were shadows everywhere, and noises in the forest, and all I could think about as I crept along was that stupid werewolf story. I picked up my pace and tried instead to think about how unrealistic it had been. Then again, four months ago I would have said the idea that secret agents were working in my school was just as farfetched.

I reached the bus and walked around to the side facing the dark forest. Agent Blue was already there waiting for me, a dark silhouette in the faint light.

"Agent Zero," he whispered.

"Hey," I said.

"You weren't followed?" he asked.

I shook my head.

"You're sure?"

"No. But I don't think I was."

"Wait here," he said, stepping around the bus. He came back twenty seconds later. "We're alone. Here."

He handed me a packet of papers and a satchel that was a little smaller than a normal backpack.

"What's this?" I asked. It was way too dark to make out any details.

"It's a map of Mount Rushmore and its trails, as well as a list of instructions detailing exactly what to do in order to get inside the base. Guard this information at all costs. It'd be better to destroy it than let anyone else discover it. Understand?"

I nodded.

"Good. The bag contains a set of vials filled with the antidote for the virus, a compact gas mask, and a few other supplies you'll probably need. Tomorrow at the monument, I'll create a diversion for you, at which point you'll slip away from the group unnoticed. Just be ready to act. Any questions so far?"

I had a thousand, but I just shook my head so he could finish the briefing.

"Much of what I'm about to say next is detailed in writing inside that packet," he said. "But I want to go over it now in case you have any vital questions regarding the mission specifics. To bypass automated security measures and get inside the base itself, there are going to be three main steps. First you'll need to locate a small crevice in the mountain under Theodore Roosevelt's face. You'll squeeze through that to find a small cave with a ventilation shaft built into the rock wall that leads to the base's power station. Getting the vent cover off is not easy, but I've included a few tools in your bag for this purpose. Once inside the vent you will need to crawl exactly one hundred and fourteen feet and then cut a hole in the bottom of the air duct shaft to access a small room underneath it. It must be exactly one hundred and fourteen feet."

"What happens if it's not?" I asked.

Even in the dark of night, I could see his expression well enough to know that I wasn't going to get an answer to that question.

"How will I measure it? And how will I cut the hole?"

"Tools," he said, pointing at the bag he'd given me. "That completes the easy part of the mission. The second phase will be to shut down the base power grid. The vital functions of the base have an emergency auxiliary power system, but most of the exterior security systems do not. Unless the main power grid is shut down, you won't have access to the labs in order to execute phase three. The power grid's manual access panel is located behind a seventeen-inch composite-steel security door. Here's where things get tricky. The only way to open the door is to simultaneously input two separate eleven-digit security codes into keypads located fifteen feet apart."

"What?" I nearly shouted. Agent Blue raised his hand

to his lips and glared at me. I continued in a harsh whisper. "That's a job for two people! How am I supposed to do that by myself?"

"Compose yourself, Zero," Agent Blue said. "It will be a challenge, but it can be done. I've included a device that might help. Besides, *difficult* has never stopped you in the past."

I just nodded, knowing that complaining would accomplish nothing but annoying my one greatest asset and supporter at the moment.

"Once you get the door open, you'll use a small device to take out the power grid," he continued. "From there, you'll need to get back into the air duct and follow it to its endpoint. This begins phase three, which will involve getting yourself across a chasm within the mountain that divides the power station from the base itself. The chasm is normally guarded by laser security beams that would have made crossing it without setting off an automated defense mechanism impossible. But by completing phase two, you will have effectively disabled the lasers. Unfortunately, they're impossible to detect, so you'll have no way to verify that they were disabled. You'll just have to trust that you followed the steps precisely for phase two."

"What happens if the beams are still active?" I asked.

Once again he gave me that look that told me I didn't want to know. But this time, I did want to know. I needed to know.

"Tell me," I insisted.

"If anything makes contact with an active laser beam, automated wall-mounted weapons with computerized heat- and motion-detecting sighting systems will eliminate the perceived security threat with extreme prejudice."

I swallowed and motioned for him to keep going.

"After getting across the chasm," Agent Blue continued, "you'll be able to access the base's ventilation system. From there, it should be a simple matter of making your way through the ducts to where Agent Nineteen and the other agents are contained. Just follow the maps and instructions provided. There is a passcode you'll need in order to enter the Jarmusch Research Lab. It's inside your mission packet, though I'd strongly suggest that you memorize it in case you lose the materials during infiltration. There is no way to override the security lock without the code. Questions?"

"Yes: Why did you even make it possible to infiltrate a secret base at all?" I said. "Isn't that a security risk in itself? Like the exhaust port in the Death Star?"

"I've never watched *Star Trek*," Agent Blue said. I didn't bother stopping him to tell him that the Death Star was actually from *Star Wars*. He was probably too busy to watch movies anyway. "But I understand your question. As you can likely deduce from the steps needed to access the base, this method is not intended to be used as an emergency entrance, and the security measures in place make a breach impossible without knowledge only the Agency can provide." He nodded at the packet with my mission instructions. "Beyond that, we didn't want to completely close off access to the base, for situations just like this one. Leaving no possible way to bypass the automated defenses in the case of a lockdown would be shortsighted."

"So you're saying there are always exceptions?" I asked. "With Agency security policies?"

"Yes," Agent Blue said.

"Even, say, breaking our cover as agents?" I asked.

"I generally don't like speaking in absolutes," Agent Blue said. "So I can't rule out the possibility that some situation could arise where an agent would need to divulge his identity to a civilian. However, that is one rule that's as close to an absolute as we have, for reasons I'm sure you of all people should understand, in the wake of the havoc that Mule Medlock has wrought on our operation. Understand me?"

I nodded, getting the distinct impression that asking the question had been a mistake. "Sorry," I mumbled.

"Do you have any other questions?"

"Yeah. I'm wondering, well . . . what are the chances I'll actually be able to pull this off?"

"Listen, Carson," Agent Blue said, putting his hand on my shoulder. His voice was more relaxed, losing a bit of the tough-guy attitude he always had when he was in agent mode. "The odds don't matter. What matters is that you *are* going to succeed. I know that when the life of a friend is on the line, you're not going to back down or give up."

I nodded. He glanced at his watch, a reminder that we were running out of time.

"Okay," he said. "Now, last thing. There is an airlock release code that you'll need to memorize. Infected personnel will likely be locked inside a secure, quarantined section of the lab itself. It will need to be manually unlocked from the outside. The code is *not* written down anywhere, nor can you write it down. You *must* memorize it, here and now. Ready?"

"Why? Why are all the others written down and not

this one?" I asked, suddenly very nervous. I never was very good with numbers.

"In the possible scenario that a double-agent back at HQ gained access to the mission briefing I just handed you and the base was infiltrated by hostiles, this code will be the only thing standing between them and access to the virus."

Even though saving Nineteen and the other agents was my mission, there were clearly still larger things at stake here.

Agent Blue nodded, satisfied that I understood the import of what he was about to tell me. "Here's the code," he said, not even waiting for me to process what he'd just said. "Four-four-seven-one-seven-zero-six five-nine-six."

"That's a lot of numbers," I said.

"It's the same as a phone number, Agent Zero," he hissed. "We don't have time for complaining, so listen."

He repeated the code again. And again. I did my best to listen and picture the numbers in my head. Usually I just saved numbers in my cell phone. I never had to memorize them.

"Say it back to me," he said.

"Four-four-seven-one-seven-zero . . ." I closed my eyes and tried to picture the numbers written down.

". . . six-five-nine-six?"

"That's it. Keep repeating that to yourself in your head tonight. Also be sure to review your map and mission parameters until you know them by heart. And wear your climbing shoes, as you'll be doing some light bouldering. Zero, this is—"

He stopped talking. His eyes widened and then he scowled.

"Someone is coming," he said. "Get back to your tent."

Before I could reply he was gone, back around the opposite side of the bus and into the trees behind it. I turned and started walking slowly back toward the bathroom, shoving the small packet of papers into the pocket of my pajama pants and slinging the bag of supplies over my shoulder while going over the passcode in my head several times. *Four-four-zero-seven-Wait-that's-not-right-oh-no-I-already-forgot-it!* Panic erupted inside my body, feeling very real, very present, like it had actual hands that were choking me.

"Carson?" a voice whispered.

"Jake?" That must have been who Agent Blue had heard. "What are you doing all the way over here?"

"I came out of the bathroom and you were gone," he said. "I went back to the tent, but you weren't there either.

Why are *you* over here? And who were you talking to just a second ago?"

"Nobody," I said.

"No, I heard it. You were talking to someone. Is everything okay?"

"I was just . . ." I glanced down, struggling to come up with yet another believable lie. "Let's go back to the tent. I'll explain along the way."

"Okay . . . ," he said. I'm pretty sure he knew I was hiding something, but he turned and followed me back toward the tent regardless.

"Was that one of the teachers?" he asked. "What were you talking about? And what's in that bag? You didn't have it when you left the tent."

My mind raced as I tried to come up with some kind of story. Instead my thoughts drifted back toward the code. I needed to remember it now or it'd be gone forever. *Focus, Carson!* The whole thing had had a nice rhythm. Four-four-seven-one-seven-zero-six-five-nine-six. That was it. Or, at least, I hoped it was. There was no way I could confirm that now, a thought that once again sent my mind reeling.

"Hello, earth to Carson," Jake said, waving a hand in front of my face. "What's going on?"

I cast about for some kind of explanation, and the thought jumped into my head again: What if I just told Jake the truth? I didn't know him all that well, but he had caught me red-handed, so lying would likely only make him more suspicious. And if I told him a bit about what was going on, I bet he could help me sneak away from the pack tomorrow when Agent Blue created a diversion. Most of all, I couldn't help but think about how great it would be to finally unload some of this stuff to somebody. All the lies were starting to tie my brain in knots.

But, no, that wasn't an option. Once again, I was being selfish, making excuses for bringing someone else into this mess. And why? Just so I wouldn't feel so alone? If I cared at all about Jake, or Dillon, or Danielle, there was only one choice, and that was to go it alone. I wasn't just protecting myself and the Agency. I was protecting them.

"Okay, see, the thing is . . . ," I began. "I had to go to the bathroom, too. But . . . I can't go around other people. So I snuck out here to go in the woods. I've always wanted to do that at least once anyway."

"What about the bag?" he asked.

"I can only use a special kind of toilet paper. I have a pretty sensitive butt. It's a long story; my whole family has a long genetic history of sensitive butts going back to my great-great-grandpa, Charlie. Soft-Cheek Charlie they used to call him at school, I guess. I was afraid that the stuff in the bathroom wouldn't be the kind I need. I hid it when we left the tent because I didn't want anyone to know."

"Okay . . . ," he said. "But who were you talking to?"

"Nobody," I said. Jake gave me a quizzical look, but I had the feeling my story was just crazy enough to be believable. And that somehow made the lies easier. "I was just talking to myself. I was getting freaked out being alone, and when I get that nervous I like to talk to myself. It's weird, I know, but it helps to calm me down. I even use different voices sometimes."

"You're right," Jake said, a smile creeping onto his face. "That's weird. Super, super weird."

We walked in silence for a while until the tents were in sight. The whole time I kept repeating the code back to myself again and again in my head. It was actually sort of nice to have that to focus on; that way I wasn't thinking about all the other crazy, dangerous, insanely difficult-sounding steps of the mission ahead.

"Look," I whispered as we approached our tent, "I'm really embarrassed about the toilet paper thing. Please don't say anything? Not even Dillon knows this secret."

"Sure," he said. "If you don't tell everyone about me saving the world in the middle of the night, we have a deal."

We bumped our knuckles together. Then we crawled back inside our tent as quietly as we could. Dillon sat up and looked at us both with a dazed, half-asleep expression.

"What were you guys out doing?" he mumbled. "Hunting for ManBearPig? Al Gore would be thrilled. I'm super serial."

Jake and I looked at each other and snorted as Dillon settled back inside his sleeping bag. Sleep-talking Dillon was even funnier than conscious Dillon, probably because he quotes *South Park* episodes instead of his own insane theories. Then Jake and I both got into our own sleeping bags. And, in spite of everything, I somehow slept soundly that night.

CHAPTER 17

BULGARIAN COOKBOOKS

T HE BUS RIDE TO MOUNT RUSHMORE THE NEXT MORNING TOOK just twenty minutes. According to Danielle, it was toward the end of the tourist season in the Black Hills, which explained why traffic was so light. Plus, it was still pretty early in the day, and I knew from past family vacations that the earlier you did stuff, the less people there would be to fight through.

After packing up my stuff and helping to take down our tent earlier that morning, I'd snuck away into the fourth stall of the campground bathroom, where I unfolded and reviewed the mission maps and details and checked the supplies I'd been given.

The moment I had opened the bag, I felt more nervous than I ever had before.

For one thing, I'd found a long retractable steel rod. This was marked as the tool that would help me input the two passcodes simultaneously. Agent Blue had to be kidding, right? I was right-handed. Like, super right-handed. My left hand was so uncoordinated, it was basically useless on its own. In fourth grade I broke my right wrist doing an impression of an injured quail (it's a long story), and I had so much trouble doing things with my left hand that the teacher made Danielle feed me by hand during lunch and write out my answers during quizzes. Not only that, but who can hold a fifteen-foot rod steady enough to input a code correctly while simultaneously inputting another code with the other hand? It was ridiculous. The mission was already over, as far as I was concerned.

And then there were the base blueprints. They were huge, and so detailed that it looked like a geometry wizard had simply barfed straight lines all over a giant sheet of drafting paper. I might as well have been trying to read a Bulgarian cookbook. In fact, I probably would have a much easier time trying to read traditional Bulgarian than trying to decipher the base's layout. I just had to hope that it would make more sense once I was actually inside the base. *If* that ever happened.

The topographical map showing the elevation and trails leading up to the foundation of the Rushmore sculptures was a little bit more straightforward. So at least there was that. And it had been pretty easy to figure out what the rest of the devices were for and how they worked. But at the same time all I could think about on that bus ride was: How could they entrust this whole mission to me? And how could they give me all these instructions just a few hours before I was supposed to do all of this?

Thankfully, Agent Blue had included a small sheet of instructions that broke down where I needed to go and what I needed to do into manageable steps. That certainly eased my anxiety just enough to keep me from going into shock and passing out in the back of the bus.

The main points of my mission:

1. Leave group once diversion is executed
2. Scale Mount Rushmore
3. Find a narrow crevice in the rock under Roosevelt's chin

4. Locate and remove exhaust vent cover
5. Crawl exact distance indicated on schematic and cut hole in duct
6. Drop into room and enter two passcodes simultaneously to open the security door
7. Disable the power grid generator
8. Climb back into vent and proceed to chasm
9. Traverse chasm to air duct on opposite side
10. Use blueprints to locate Jarmusch Research Lab and enter through security door
11. Locate six to ten base personnel, verify whether they are alive or dead
12. Use high-security code to release the secure airlock
13. Administer antidote as needed
14. Assist in Romero Virus security and base evacuation as needed
15. If all else fails, refer to the instructions on how to initiate the Base Security Breach Self-Destruct Sequence

Simple. Right? Just fifteen simple steps to save the world.

As the bus drove up the winding path toward the huge parking ramp at Mount Rushmore, everyone around me buzzed with excitement. Most of us had never seen the monument before, at least not in real life. Had I not been so distracted worrying about my mission, I'd have been pretty excited myself.

We pulled onto a huge parking ramp and then walked up wide granite stairs toward the monument visitor center. Tons of flags and plaques lined the walkway. It was all pretty impressive. I figured that we'd just be pulling over on some hillside and there would be Washington's face and Jefferson's and the rest of them carved into a mountain in the middle of nowhere. But it wasn't like that at all. The visitor center was huge and impressive. The gift shop alone was almost as big as my whole house. And the entire park was packed with people despite it being early in the morning and near the end of tourist season.

The chaperones tried to keep us corralled as we all headed down the long concrete path toward the monument itself. We bypassed the visitor center and gift shop and headed right to the initial viewing area.

Then, finally, we saw the monument. Four massive presidential faces peered out into the Black Hills from a mountainside high above us. It was a pretty amazing sight. I couldn't believe how intricate the carvings were. Even the pictures I'd seen couldn't have prepared me for how cool and detailed the monument looked in person.

"It's way smaller than I expected," one girl complained.

"Yeah, no kidding," Dillon agreed. "Especially since I know there's a secret vault filled with gold stashed inside Lincoln's face."

"Don't worry, we'll be taking that hiking trail to get a closer look," said Mr. Gist. "After a quick bathroom break, that is."

I looked down below into the shallow valley where he was pointing. There was a hiking trail leading up to a series of wooden platforms and steps that winded their way partially up the hillside toward the monument itself. It ended a little under a quarter of the way up to the base of the faces. After that, the hillside got much steeper and rockier. That was the terrain I was going to have to climb. I glanced over at Mr. Jensen, who was looking at me meaningfully.

I tried to swallow, but my throat was suddenly broken. This just kept feeling more and more impossible with each passing minute. I was now convinced that Agent Nineteen and all the other agents trapped inside were going to die that day. And it would be my fault.

010101010101010101001100101010101010101010101
010101010101010000101001010101001010101010
101010000100101001010101001010101010101010
000010101010101010011001   10101
001010110101000100101   100
1010100001001010010   010

CHAPTER 18

MOUNT RUSHMORE IS FILTHY

"**M**AN, THIS IS . . . NOT WHAT I . . . EXPECTED," OLIVER SAID, panting as we ascended a series of wooden staircases and concrete walkways leading farther up the mountainside.

Oliver was by far the heaviest kid on the trip. But to be fair, even I had to admit that it was a ton of steps up to the highest public-viewing point. We were almost to the top of the man-made trail now, and I did my best to stay at the back of the pack so I could sneak away unnoticed when Agent Blue finally initiated his diversion.

The only kids near the back with me were Oliver,

Dillon, and Jake. It made me nervous since it might be kind of hard to shake my two friends unless Agent Blue's distraction was particularly spectacular. Then again, most of their attention was on scanning the forest around us for signs of Smallfoot.

Danielle was sticking near the front of the group, partially so she could ingest all the information that the three chaperones were dispensing along the way, and also partially, I suspected, because she was annoyed that Jake and Dillon were hanging out so much. I couldn't really figure out her problem with Jake. He had taken the fall for Prankpocalypse, after all. And it was usually Dillon who had a harder time trusting and welcoming new kids into our group of friends.

According to my watch, I now had two hours left to find Agent Nineteen and help him. If Agent Blue was going to make his move, he'd better do it soon. I'd been watching him the whole time, and he was doing a pretty good job of pretending like he was just a chaperone on a school trip. He'd been basically ignoring me the entire hike. Which was probably a lot smarter than what I was doing: making it all kinds of obvious by staring at him constantly. But I couldn't help it. I was nervous.

We got to the top platform and everyone looked up

inside the former presidents' nostrils for a while, made some funny comments, listened to the chaperones doling out more information and took notes in their journals, and then eventually started back down the trail. Was Agent Blue ever going to make the diversion? Had he already done it, and I'd missed it?

But it was then that I realized he'd been waiting for a reason. He might as well wait until everyone was heading down so that me being in the back of the pack would also mean I was higher up the hillside than everyone else. It was smart.

As we started down the trail, Mr. Jensen launched into another informative speech about the monument.

"It took fourteen years and four hundred workers to carve the monument," he said. "Many people worry that it will eventually erode, but it actually only erodes about one inch every ten thousand years. In fact, the mountain was only ever cleaned once, by a manufacturer of cleaning machines who did it for free."

"Man," Oliver breathed hard, hunched over next to me. Could seventh graders have heart attacks? I wasn't sure, but with how red and glossy his pudgy face looked, it certainly seemed possible. His face resembled the honey-glazed hams my mom sometimes made on holidays. It was making me uncomfortable.

"Come on, the way back down will be a lot easier," Dillon said, putting an arm around Oliver's shoulder.

I was now dead last as the group continued down the trail, with Jake, Oliver, and Dillon just a few steps in front of me. And I knew the diversion would be coming soon. What I didn't know was that it had already happened.

It just took me a few extra seconds to notice.

CHAPTER 19

IN TEDDY ROOSEVELT'S SHADOW

HEARD THE SHOUTING FIRST. THEN I SAW MR. JENSEN LEANING over the railing, continuing his string of yelling, which was obviously causing even more of a commotion among the kids since it was coming from a teacher. Everyone rushed over to see what had happened.

"I dropped my camera!" he yelled.

This was my moment. All I saw were backs of heads as everyone hurried over to see the damage. I ducked under the wooden railing and quickly hopped down onto the hillside. The wooden staircase was slightly elevated in most spots to keep it as flat as possible, which worked to my advantage since I was able to stay under it and out of sight as I scrambled back up the hillside through crunchy late fall brush.

There were a few boulders and stones to get over, and I dashed as far and as fast as I could. I didn't bother looking back until I was at least fifty yards past the end of the wooden trail. Then I dived behind a huge evergreen tree to catch my breath.

Slowly, I poked my head around the trunk and looked back down toward our field trip group. They were still gathered on the platform where Mr. Jensen had "accidentally" dropped his camera. They looked shockingly small from up here. Most of the kids were still peering over the side of the rail. As far as I could tell, nobody had a clue that I was gone. I steeled myself and continued working my way up the hillside, making sure to keep behind as many trees as possible.

The going got steeper and rockier as I went. But I kept moving, despite my aching muscles. After several minutes, I was now actively climbing on all fours. In fact, it was so steep that if I tried to stand on just two feet, I'd probably tumble over backward and roll down the hill.

I wanted desperately to look back, but knew the view

would only make me more nervous. So I kept facing forward, looking up at the four massive stone faces above me. Their chins were getting surprisingly close. But that also meant the mountainside was getting a whole lot steeper. Which meant there were fewer trees to hide behind.

Nevertheless, I pushed on. A few minutes later, I reached a huge boulder that formed a sort of ledge. I climbed up onto it and then knelt down to once again catch my breath. Sweat soaked the clothes underneath my jacket and dripped through my bangs and into my eyes. I wiped it away with my sleeve.

My countdown watch indicated I had just over an hour left.

I checked my maps. My entry point was underneath Teddy Roosevelt's face. The problem was what stood between me and old Ted: sheer cliffs, massive boulders, and terrain so steep I didn't think I could climb it. There appeared to be a clear trail on the map, but I had no idea if I was on it, or how to get to it if I wasn't. The topographical maps had been a lot easier to read when I wasn't standing in the middle of the area they depicted.

Eventually, I decided to stick to paths I could see that seemed the least likely to get me killed. I put the maps away and then crawled to the edge of the boulder and peeked down.

I couldn't even see the wooden stairs of the tourist path. It was completely obstructed by trees and rocks and the angle of the hill. At least I didn't have to worry about being spotted by the group anymore. People down at the viewing center might be able to spot me if they were looking through the coin-operated binoculars. But I couldn't worry about that now; all that mattered was getting to Agent Nineteen as soon as possible.

Using tree roots and larger rocks as handholds, I started climbing once again. I was so close to the faces now they were nothing more than huge, smooth stone outcroppings.

My focus remained on making sure I always had something solid to grab and somewhere to lodge my toes. I was so focused on those two things that it caught me by surprise when I looked up and realized that I was just twenty feet or so from the underside of the presidents' faces. Twenty feet from somehow surviving this climb.

I'd passed the last of the trees now. All that stood between me and the base's secret entrance was one last cliff off to the right of Lincoln's face. Once I was under his chin, I'd be able to crawl my way toward Teddy Roosevelt, who was tucked farther back into the mountain.

Being so close seemed to remotivate me despite how exhausted I felt, despite the fact that the next few phases of the mission would be even more difficult.

I resumed climbing. Every time I was convinced that I'd just found the last good grip or foot ledge, I'd locate another, then another. Before I knew it, I was just a few feet from the top. My arms were hurting so badly they were going numb. But I pushed on.

Or, at least I tried to. The moment I reached up for the next little ledge, my foot slipped and I began to fall.

101010101010100001010010101010010101010100
0101000010010100101010010101010101010101
0001 0011001010101010101010
010 001010101001010101001
01 1010100101010101010101
10 1100101010101010101010

CHAPTER 20

CARSON JUST DIED?

OKAY, I DIDN'T ACTUALLY FALL TO MY DEATH.

Instead, I managed to somehow hang on with both hands. But as tired as my raw fingers and aching arm muscles were, I knew it was only a matter of time before I did actually fall.

I kicked my feet along the cliff, searching for any sort of foothold as my fingers already started slipping off the rock ledge above me. It was all I could do to not look down and pee my pants. I felt my throat close up and I flailed my legs wildly.

My feet found nothing to anchor to, and my heart sank. I'd been so close. Just a few feet from the top. But there was no way I'd make it now. My fingers continued slipping and I knew I was likely seconds from imminent death.

But then suddenly a hand came out of nowhere and grabbed one of my wrists. Then another hand grabbed my other one. The hands were small, but surprisingly strong.

"Come on, I'll pull, but you got to kick!" a voice yelled out from above me.

And so I did. I dug my feet into the cliff and pushed up as my savior pulled. I heard a loud grunt and before I knew it I was on top of the cliff, sprawled on the grainy stone ground.

I lay there facedown for a few moments trying to figure out if I was actually still alive. Then I looked up to see who had saved my life.

Jake sat just a few feet away, breathing hard.

"What . . ." is all I managed to say.

"That was close," he said, climbing to his feet.

He held out a hand and helped pull me up. My legs felt unstable and wobbly, like those of someone trying to use crutches for the very first time. The adrenaline from almost dying made me feel like I'd just ingested eighteen pounds of pure sugar. My arms and hands were vibrating.

"You saved me," I said. "How . . . ?"

"I saw you sneak off and so I followed you." He shrugged and smiled. "After last night, I could tell you were up to something. Lucky for you, right?"

My brain tried to register what he was saying, but something else was bothering me even more than all of that.

"But how in the world did you get past me and beat me up here?" I said.

"There's a much easier path over there, with way less climbing." He pointed across the ledge over toward the base of Washington's face. "I lost you along the way and figured you were still in front of me. Then I got up here and didn't see you. That's when I heard you yelling."

"I was yelling?" I said. I didn't remember yelling.

"Yeah, you were screaming," he said with a grin.

I just shook my head. I guess that would have been the benefit of being able to read that stupid map once I got up here. It likely would have directed me to the easier path.

"How did you get away from the group?" I asked.

"Dillon was busy explaining to Oliver the importance of eating kale. I don't think he noticed when I left."

I nodded. Dillon *loved* kale. He called it the MVP of the American Food Revolution and would always lecture me about how it's secretly the only truly healthy natural food in existence, and how the government doesn't want us to know about it so they can make money off our unhealthy lifestyles. Or something like that.

"So, what are you up to?" Jake asked. "A prank?"

"Well, not exactly . . ."

"You might as well tell me now and let me help," he said.

I sighed. *Here we go again*, I thought. Telling Jake the truth would be breaking the number-one most important rule of being a secret agent. And not only would I be doing that, but I'd be helping an outsider infiltrate a secret Agency base. Director Isadoris and Agent Blue would be furious, even if I did somehow manage to successfully complete my mission.

Still, it was impossible to deny that having him along for the mission would make things loads easier. Him saving my life a minute ago was proof enough of that. I began to sweat. I didn't know what to do, and Jake was growing more and more confused by the minute. Could I really tell him what was going on?

I laid out the facts in my head:

Jake had just caught me red-handed. The only real alternative to blowing my cover would be to throw him off the cliff, which I didn't think I was even physically capable of doing, let alone would ever want to.

Jake would make phase two of the base infiltration a million times easier. Scratch that: He'd make it *possible*. I still had no clue how I was going to input the two codes simultaneously. Using the extendable rod was ridiculous, and yet it was still my best option unless I could figure out how to push buttons telekinetically in the next few minutes. If I was being realistic, bringing Jake along was the only way to be sure that part of the mission would go as planned.

Agent Nineteen was going to die in forty-five minutes, and the clock was continuing to tick as I stood there debating this whole thing.

It really all boiled down to one question. What was worse: exposing my cover, or letting everyone inside the base die and possibly allowing a deadly apocalyptic virus to escape containment?

When considered that way, it was no choice at all.

"Okay, here's the thing," I said. "I'm on my way to save the lives of several government agents, and prevent the outbreak of an engineered bioweapon, all of which are contained in a top secret lab hidden inside Mount Rushmore."

The look on Jake's face was so priceless, I almost laughed.

"I know this sounds ridiculous," I started, "and even if you don't believe me at all, I don't care because I need your help either way. Basically, the long and short of it is that there's a secret government agency operating in Minnow and they've hired me to break into one of their secret laboratories here. There was a virus outbreak and I need to get inside to deliver the cure."

Jake finally broke his silence. He laughed. But as he kept staring at me, the laughter slowly subsided.

He didn't believe me. I wouldn't have believed me either. But as I stood there with him, I couldn't help but notice how amazing it felt to finally be able to come clean to someone. It was like there had been a relentless buzzing noise inside my brain, and now, suddenly, it was gone. The air felt cleaner, easier to breathe.

"I know," I said. "It's quite a story. But if you come along with me now, and you promise to help me, I'll prove it to you."

He smiled again, but more cautiously. "Sure, man. I'll go along with this."

"Okay then," I said. "Follow me."

We moved around to the base of Roosevelt's face and I took out the blueprints and map that Agent Blue had given me. The map was directing me toward a crevice somewhere around that area.

"And this 'Agency' . . . they hired you to do this job why?" Jake asked, clearly struggling to wrap his head around the story.

"There's not a lot of time to explain," I said. "But mostly, they didn't know which agents of theirs they could trust, and they needed someone who had a believable reason to be at Mount Rushmore on this particular day. Now: We need to find some sort of crevice around here, one we can crawl into."

I ran my hand along the smooth rock. There were plenty of cracks and crevices, but none that looked large enough to fit a textbook into, let alone a thirteen-year-old kid. We kept walking along the wall of the mountainside. The ledge we were on got deeper as we went farther back toward where President Roosevelt's Adam's apple would have been, had they carved that part out.

"You're messing with me," Jake said. "There is no way this is real."

"In about five seconds, I'm going to show you that it

is," I said, finally starting to relax a bit. I still wasn't sure that telling Jake was the right move, but now that I'd done it, I was feeling a million times better about the task at hand. "Here, look at this," I said, handing the detailed, complex base blueprint to Jake.

His eyes went wide, and his jaw hung open. "What is this?" he said, trying to collect himself. "If this is a prank or joke, then it's the most elaborate prank in history!"

"It's crazy," I said, nodding. "But true."

"Yeah," he said. "And the craziest part is that I think I'm actually starting to believe you."

He seemed surprised at the words coming out of his own mouth. Then he shrugged and nodded with a grin, as if to tell himself it was okay to believe me. And as he did so, I finally found what I was looking for. It didn't look like much until you were basically right on top of it. I wouldn't have even seen it at all if I hadn't taken out the flashlight my mom had bought for me at Wal-Mart. But the crevice was there, just like it was supposed to be. A vertical, narrow crack in the rock, maybe seven feet tall and ten inches to a foot wide.

An adult would never be able to squeeze into it. But a lanky seventh grader just might. Or so I hoped. The whole mission hinged on it.

"You're going in there?" Jake asked, peering into the depths of the crevice.

"Yup," I said. "*We* are."

He gulped.

I checked my countdown watch: *00:42:39.*

My flashlight beam wasn't strong enough to see what was beyond the first seven feet or so of the crevice. After putting the flashlight in my mouth, I took off my backpack and turned sideways, holding it next to my body. Then I squeezed myself into the crack. My butt scraped against the side of the rock and I hit my head a few times, but I was just barely able to fit if I kept my head turned to the side. I took short, choppy side steps as I inched farther and farther in. Slobber dripped out of the corners of my open mouth as I kept the flashlight gripped between my teeth.

Jake grunted behind me, struggling to squeeze himself into the crevice. We were about the same size, but he was a little taller and apparently a little thicker as well.

We inched our way deeper and deeper into the mountain. It was dark, cold, and tight. For a short time I was convinced I couldn't breathe and dropped the flashlight. The crevice was thrust into darkness, and there was no chance I could bend over far enough to retrieve the flashlight. Several times, I was convinced I felt spiders crawling across my face. It was enough to make me almost have a panic attack and just give up.

But Jake kept urging me to keep going.

"It has to end, it has to end," he kept saying, although it sounded as though he could barely breathe himself.

But he was right. Eventually it did end. I took another few steps and then I was once again out in the open. It was still pitch-black, but at least I was free from the clutches of the crevice that I had been convinced would become my stone coffin.

Jake stumbled into whatever room we were in and crashed into me. We both went sprawling to the solid rock floor. It was darker than dark. I mean, the insides of eyelids were more colorful and bright than what I was seeing just then.

"Sorry," Jake said from the ground next to me. "You okay?"

"Yeah," I said, scared to move, not knowing what was around me.

"What now?" Jake asked. "Got another flashlight?"

"Nope," I said, realizing that without a light the mission was once again on the brink of failure.

0000101010101010101001100101010101010101
010101010101000010100101010010101010100
101010000100101001010100101010101010
00001   001100101010101010101010
0010   010101010010101010100
101   CHAPTER 21   01010100101010101010
000   10010101010101010101

A FRUIT ROLL-UP SAVES
THE WORLD

WE JUST SAT THERE FOR A FEW MINUTES. WITHOUT A LIGHT I couldn't read my instructions, or the map, or see where the heck we were supposed to go next. I remembered from the mission briefing earlier that morning that I was now at phase one of the base infiltration, which meant there was an exhaust vent that we needed to find. But it might take hours to find without being able to see. We didn't have hours. We had minutes.

"What about your phone?" Jake asked.

Duh.

I took my phone from my pocket and pressed the home button. A pale blue glow lit up our faces. Jake's was completely coated in dirt and dust. I could only imagine that mine was as well.

A glance at my countdown watch told me we had just thirty-nine minutes left.

I switched my phone to flashlight mode and pointed the light up. It was powerful enough to illuminate the little entryway we had fallen into. It was about the size of Mr. Gomez's small office.

As I moved the light beam around the cave, it didn't take long to find the exhaust vent that Agent Blue had written about in my instructions. It was a grate about a foot and a half tall and two feet wide near the base of the cave wall opposite the crevice opening.

I flashed the light inside the vent. It was made of metal and full of dust and dirt particles. But it was definitely wide enough for us to squeeze through. The problem was that there were no screws or any visible seams.

I handed my phone to Jake and grabbed the vent cover. I pulled, but it didn't budge. It felt as if it were welded into the stone around it.

"How do we get in?" Jake asked.

"Shine that over here," I said, unzipping my backpack.

I dug around through the supplies Agent Blue had included there. I thought I remembered seeing several fruit roll-ups earlier. I didn't need to be told what those were, not after my last stint with the Agency. It didn't take long to find one near the bottom.

"Isn't it an odd time for a snack?" Jake asked.

"Bring the light over here," I instructed.

After unwrapping the roll-up, I stretched it out until it tore in the middle. I kept pulling at the sides until I eventually had a flimsy hoop of fake fruit. I began stuffing it into the spaces where the sides of the vent met the rock until it formed a kind of red frame around the vent cover.

"Uhh, okay," Jake said, clearly confused.

I located the detonator and then scooted to the opposite side of the cave.

"You might want to join me over here," I said.

Jake followed my lead and ducked as I covered my head with my arms, plugging one ear with my left index finger. With my right hand I pressed the detonator button.

The fruit-roll-up explosive was normally not very loud, but inside the small cave, it was almost deafening. For a second after it went off, I thought for sure that the cave might collapse. But the haze cleared out through the small crevice, and it became clear that the walls were still intact.

Fortunately, the same could not be said for the vent cover. It had blown completely off the side of the rock wall. In fact, it was now in several pieces scattered about the cave. I supposed we were probably lucky that neither of us had been hit by ventilation shrapnel.

I checked the time on my countdown watch again.

00:32:54

"Come on, we have to hurry," I said, and then dived into the open vent without even waiting for a reply.

Once inside, I searched through my bag for the laser sight Agent Blue had included. It was a small black tube barely as large as a battery with a magnetic strip attached to the side. It hadn't taken long earlier that morning in the campground bathroom to figure out how to use it.

I turned a small dial on top of the tube until the tiny digital display read *114.* Then I stuck it on the lip of the air-duct opening. A laser illuminated the floor of the air duct with a red line, marking off the feet with little notches.

"Whoa!" Jake said. "What is that?"

"Just a little gadget they provided to help," I said,

trying to play it off casually, even though I also thought the device was incredibly cool.

Jake followed me through the metal vent. It felt wide enough to fit a train compared to the tight death trap that had been the mountain crevice. We crawled for a few minutes until we got to where the red laser notches stopped. It was marked with a little symbol next to a red digital readout: *114 ft.*

"This is it," I said.

"What now?"

Instead of answering, I took my bag of supplies off my shoulder and located another small device using my phone light.

The laser cutter had been fairly simple to figure out that morning. I did feel a little guilty about the wallet-size chunk of the fourth stall in the campground bathroom that was now missing. I hadn't realized just how easily the cutter could slice through metal until I tested it out.

The device looked like a cordless power drill, except a lot smaller. And instead of spinning when I pressed the trigger, the end emitted a glowing green beam of who-knows-what about half an inch long. It wasn't like welding, either; when it contacted the metal of the air-duct shaft, it didn't give off a blinding light or even create sparks. It simply passed right through it with ease, as if I were cutting a wet napkin with a razor blade.

I sliced out a rough four-foot circle around the spot the red laser sight indicated was 114 feet. Once I finished cutting, the circle of air duct fell away and I heard a loud clatter just below. The room I'd cut into was completely dark.

The duct crinkled and dented under my weight as I swung my legs into the hole so I was basically sitting on the edge.

"How far down is it?" Jake asked.

"I don't know. It sounded like it wasn't too far when the chunk fell," I said. "I'm going to jump."

"Wait!" Jake said. "What about that laser-distance thing—do we leave it there?"

"We're coming back up after we do this," I said. "We can grab it then if there's time."

"How will we get back up?"

"I've got a device that can help us," I said, patting my backpack.

Jake nodded.

"Okay, here goes nothing," I said, and lowered myself into the black abyss.

0000101010101010101010011001010101010101010
010101010101010000101001010101001010101010
101010000100101001010101001010101010101010
00001   1001100101010101010101
0010   0010101010010101010100
101   CHAPTER 22   1010100101010101010
000   1001010101010101010101

WHEN HAVING NO RHYTHM
IS THE END OF THE WORLD

HELD ON TO THE LIP OF THE AIR DUCT VENT UNTIL I WAS dangling from the hole. I closed my eyes—not that it mattered since I couldn't see anything—and let go. I knew that when falling, the key was to stay limp, don't tense up. Keep your knees and legs loose and try to roll on landing.

The ground came a lot sooner than I expected, which caught me off guard, and instead of rolling while falling to the ground, I landed on my feet and stumbled forward right into a solid, hard surface. I bounced off it face-first and landed on my butt.

"Oh, man!" Jake said from above me. "Are you okay? That didn't sound good. What happened? I'm coming down."

"Wait," I said, thankful that I hadn't hurt my brain too badly to speak despite the pounding headache. "Hang on, I'll help. It's not that far of a drop."

I climbed to my feet and felt my aching forehead. There was already a small lump forming above my eyebrow. As a prankster, I'd had my fair share of bumps and scrapes over the years. This was far from the worst injury I'd suffered. Not that it didn't still hurt.

"Okay, lower yourself down," I said as I switched on my phone flashlight again.

The air duct was only a few feet above my head, attached to a low concrete ceiling. Jake's legs poked through the hole a few moments later and he lowered himself. I grabbed his ankles and eased him down.

"Thanks," he said. We both checked out the surroundings. We were in a room a bit larger than the cave entrance. It was empty aside from the air duct running along the ceiling and a few smaller tubes connected to it from the far wall. Three of the four walls were concrete and one was made of metal. There were two small keypads on the ends of the metal wall.

"Well, looks like we're right where we need to be," I said.

I rummaged inside my bag and found the sheet with the two security codes written on it. I tore it in half and handed the side labeled *left pad (facing door)* to Jake. I took the right pad. The codes were each eleven digits long.

"Okay," I said as we each walked over to face our own keypads. "According to the instructions, each number needs to be pressed within half a second of the other, including the last number. And the whole thing needs to be input in less than eleven seconds total, so we can't go very slow. Let's do a dry test run on the wall next to the pad, okay?"

Jake nodded.

"Ready, steady, go."

We each air pressed our codes into the wall next to the keypads. He finished a full two seconds ahead of me. This was still going to be a lot harder than I expected, even with help. I couldn't imagine trying to do this alone with just a long metal rod.

We practiced it two more times, and on the last try we finished pretty much simultaneously.

"What happens if we're off?" Jake asked.

I shook my head. "Let's just not be. Ready for real now?"

Jake nodded.

"Ready, steady, go," I said again.

We entered the codes just as we had practiced. Nothing happened for several seconds, and then an automated voice filled the small room.

"Unauthorized access attempt detected," the voice said. "Only one attempt remains before automated security enforcement commences."

"That doesn't sound good," I said.

As soon as the words left my mouth, several dozen panels in the concrete walls, floor, and ceiling slid open all around us. The openings were small, maybe the size of a playing card, and we couldn't see what was in them. They just looked like little menacing black eyes staring us down from all sides. I knew that they were not there to cheer us on. Or tell us tough luck if we messed up a second time. I was fairly certain that if we messed up again, these little black holes would be the last things either of us ever saw. Jake's expression told me he had a similar suspicion.

"What went wrong?" he asked.

"We must have been off. Or maybe one of us missed a number," I said. "We need to work out a better system."

We spent the next few minutes working out a timing rhythm where we actually counted out a steady beat. Which is harder than it sounds, counting out a beat while pressing different numbers than the ones you're counting in your head at the same time. But after a dozen dry runs on the blank wall next to the keypads, the beat was coming naturally and we didn't need to count it out loud anymore.

We were down to twenty-three minutes. We couldn't risk delaying any further; we had to try it now. I took a deep breath and looked at Jake.

"Are you sure you want to do this?" I said. "I won't blame you if you want to back out now. Really."

"You said if we don't do this a deadly virus could get out, right?" he asked.

"Yup."

"Good enough for me," he said. "On your count."

We took our positions and started tapping out the beat on the wall next to the pad. My nerves flared and my hand shook. One missed button and we were likely toast. I forced myself to calm down as we tapped the wall in unison.

"Okay, after three, go!" I said.

We typed in our numbers to a steady rhythm, which was slightly different than merely pretending on a blank wall. However, we'd practiced enough times and enough was on the line that I think we both just got into a zone. We finished at exactly the same time and then both instinctively ducked.

But no hail of bullets or streams of flame or plumes of deadly vapor released from the holes in the wall. Instead, there was a loud clank, followed by the sound of hydraulics within the walls working to open a metal door that probably weighed a gazillion tons. The metal door parted, sliding into the walls, revealing a huge computerized control panel the size of four classroom Smart Boards put together. There were switches, blinking lights, dials, knobs, and more. But none of that mattered since I was there to disable it, not operate it.

"Wow," Jake said. "What now?"

"Well," I said, digging through my bag, "according to the mission documents, an EMP should be able to disable this thing without causing a cave-in."

"EMP?"

"Electromagnetic pulse." I pulled the small device from the bag. It looked like a slightly oversize harmonica with a few switches and backlit buttons. "Supposedly this thing takes out any electrical device nearby when activated."

"Cool," Jake said.

I held it up toward the center of the large transformer control panel and it flew from my hand and attached itself to the metal surface as the powerful magnet backing kicked in. I had a feeling that I wouldn't be able to remove it even if I wanted to. I held up the small wireless detonator.

"How far away do we need to be?" Jake asked.

"I don't know. The instructions didn't say," I said nervously. "Let's go stand in the corner. I think the force is entirely electromagnetic, though, so we should be fine anywhere."

Jake joined me in the far corner of the small concrete room. We looked at each other anxiously. I checked my countdown watch. Nineteen minutes left. There wasn't any time to waste wondering if this was a bad idea or not.

"Okay, on three," I said.

Jake covered his ears as I counted down and then pressed the button. The "blast" was almost instantaneous. It started with a pop like a huge lightbulb going out. That was followed by a wave of nausea, coupled with an odd feeling that something bad was about to happen. A high-pitched ringing pierced my head, and then the room was pitch-black as my cell phone flashlight and the lights on the huge control panel went out all at once.

"I think I just fried my cell phone," I said, futilely pressing the On button.

"At least we know it worked," Jake said. "Though, I don't feel very well all of a sudden."

"Me, either," I said, still feeling like I wanted to puke. "I think it might have something to do with the energy field that thing generated. Or maybe we're just imagining it."

"Either way, let's get out of here," Jake said.

I nodded. Then realized he couldn't see me in the pitch-black. Not to mention I was out of flashlights.

"Help me find the bag," I said, crouching down on the concrete floor.

I heard Jake do the same and it took only a few minutes to locate the bag inside the tiny room, even without being able to see anything. I thought I remembered seeing a few plastic green tubes when I took inventory in the bathroom earlier that morning. My hands closed around one of them in the bag. I removed it and bent it hard at the middle.

A crack was followed by the sudden glow of a neon green stick.

"Ah!" I shouted as Jake's glowing green face appeared just six inches from my own.

"Sorry, I didn't know I was that close," he said, backing away.

"It's okay, just startled me," I said. "Let's get moving. We're running out of time." I glanced down at my watch to check the countdown. But the numbers were no longer glowing. The EMP must have taken that out as well.

There was no choice but to keep moving as quickly as possible.

CHAPTER 23

THE TIM TEBOW OF HEROES

AFTER I BOOSTED JAKE BACK UP INTO THE AIR DUCT, HE reached down and helped me up. He went back and retrieved the red laser sight, just in case, while I continued on in the vent. It was a straight shot to the end of the air duct, which was sealed off with another metal grate. Jake had caught up by the time I was able to knock it out with a few good kicks.

I leaned out of the opening and held out the glow stick, then gasped and almost lost my balance. Which would have resulted in me falling into a vast abyss. The chasm was a narrow crevice with no top or bottom in sight. It could have gone all the way down to the earth's core for all I knew. In the rock wall directly across the fifteen-foot gap and slightly above us was another vent cover.

"Wow," Jake said, leaning over my shoulder. "How are we gonna get across?"

"I have a grappling hook, but I only have one harness," I said. "I think I should cross, then shoot the grappling hook back to this side. Then you can attach the bag to that end and I'll tow it up. I don't want to risk dropping anything by taking it across with me."

"What about me?" Jake asked.

"You should head back," I said. "This might get even more dangerous, and I've already asked too much of you."

He hesitated, but then nodded. There was really no easy way to get us both across, not without wasting valuable time. "I'll make sure you get across safely, at least."

I took out the grappling hook, which was very similar to the one the Agency had given me earlier that year, except this one wasn't disguised as a set of keys. It was just a small hook that could be fired from a gun-like device, which could then be attached to a nylon harness.

After strapping the harness to my shoulders and

waist, I took careful aim and fired the grappling hook a few feet above the vent cover on the other side of the deep crevice. It lodged into the rock wall more or less where I'd intended.

So far, I hadn't seen one automated defense laser or turret gun, which I was hoping meant that we had successfully taken out the power grid. The grappling hook had a motorized lift so I wouldn't have to climb the wire, but I'd still have to swing across before activating it since there would be some slack in the line until I was on the other side. I didn't know what kind of rock the mountain was made of or whether the hook would hold under the pressure of my weight hitting it all at once, but there was no other option.

I handed the bag to Jake and then clamped the glow stick in my teeth. Even partially in my mouth, it was just bright enough to allow me to see the other side of the fifteen-foot abyss between where I was crouched and the ventilation shaft leading to the base interior.

"Good luck," Jake said as I clipped the grappling-hook device to my harness.

I nodded at him, took a deep breath, and then let myself fall from the vent. I swung across more smoothly than expected, dropping as the line went taut. I put out my legs in front of me and then let my knees bend as my feet connected with the rock wall on the other side of the chasm.

The impact was less violent than I anticipated. It was just like hopping down from a short fence. Still, I was dangling above a bottomless cavern with nothing but a thin wire holding me up. I stood on the rock wall, holding the grappling hook wire to steady myself. I hit the switch on the device and slowly walked up the wall, allowing the powerful motorized pulley system to do most of the heavy lifting.

Once I got to the vent I hit the switch again to stop the pulley. I tentatively touched the vent cover, half expecting it to have some sort of defense mechanism. It just felt like normal cold metal. I grabbed it and pulled. It didn't budge. There was no sign of any screws. The vent cover was firmly embedded into the rock wall just like the first one.

"What's wrong?" Jake called out.

I took the glow stick from my mouth and called back, "I can't get the cover off."

"Do you have any more of those fruit roll-up things?" he asked.

It was a good idea; I'd give him that. Except, how

would I detonate it safely while dangling here? Not that I had much choice. The clock was ticking.

"There should be two left, can you find them and toss me one?" I said.

"I'm gonna need to crack open the second glow stick. I can't see anything," Jake said.

"Okay," I called back. I didn't know how long these things lasted, but I hoped that I wouldn't really need them much after this phase in the mission anyway.

Jake opened a glow stick and then located the two fruit-roll-up explosives. I spun myself around so I was facing him.

"Okay, toss it up," I said, putting the glow stick back in my mouth.

Jake threw the fruit roll-up underhand. It floated toward me, but fell way short of my extended hand. It tumbled down into the darkness of the abyss below. Jake hadn't even come close.

I raised my head, trying not to look too annoyed.

"Sorry, I'm nervous," he said. "Plus, it's hard to judge the distance with only this neon green light. And I've never had very good aim anyway."

It was true. He'd played basketball with us several times and he was by far the worst shot in our whole group of friends. He always made up for it in pure effort and tenacity, grabbing rebounds and such, but remembering that didn't give me much confidence for the second attempt.

"Well, this is our last one, so make it count."

He nodded and took several deep breaths. He closed his eyes, trying to calm himself. Then he looked up at me again.

"Ready?"

I nodded.

He swung his arm outside of the vent and tossed the last fruit roll-up. He threw it much harder this time, but his aim was no better and the fruit roll-up sailed over my head and to the left. The throw was so bad that I knew right away I'd have no chance to catch it. Which actually was for the better, because it gave me time to spin around and kick left in hopes of catching it on the rebound after it hit the wall. Had the throw been slightly better I'd probably have wasted precious seconds trying to grab it and then had no chance at all. But, as it turned out, sometimes if you were going to miss, it was better to miss by a mile.

The fruit roll-up bounced off the wall several feet above me, and because I'd had those extra seconds to turn around and move left, I was there waiting for it as it fell. It landed right in my lap and I cupped my hands and caught it, breathing out as I clutched it tightly.

"Oh, man!" Jake said, pumping his fist. "What a catch!"

Now the real question was how to do this without blowing off one of my arms or legs. I started by unrolling the fruit explosive and stretching it around the vent cover like I had done to get inside the mountain just fifteen minutes before.

I looked at the rock walls on either side of the vent. Several feet down and to the right was a small outcropping. It definitely wasn't big enough to stand on, but if I could lower myself enough and swing over to it, I might be able to grab it and hold on just long enough to safely detonate the explosive.

"Take cover," I yelled as I hit the switch on the grappling hook to lower myself down several feet.

Holding the detonator in my left hand, I kicked away from the wall and tried to swing right toward the outcropping. I ended up just short. I tried again and got a little closer. On the third try, I managed to get a weak grip on the rock with my free hand. It was now or never. I quickly pressed the detonator.

The small explosion sounded like a nuclear blast

inside the narrow crevice. The force of it caused me to lose my grip and I immediately started swinging back toward the vent. Just as I was getting back to the opening, which no longer had a metal cover, I heard a snap above me. The wire had broken.

0101010101010101001100101010101010
0101010101010000010100101010010101010
1010100001001010010101001010101010101010
0000101010101010011001 10101
0010101101010001001 0100
1010100001001010010 010

CHAPTER 24

HAPPY BIRTHDAY, GOLLUM

SOMEHOW, I WAS JUST ABLE TO GET MY HANDS UP TO THE jagged vent opening and catch myself before falling into the abyss below. I knew my fingers wouldn't be able to hold the hard edge for long so I immediately started pulling myself up. Using my last ounce of energy, I kicked up my leg and got my knee onto the edge of the vent.

From there, I pulled myself the rest of the way up. I fell on my back inside the air duct, which was slightly larger than the one across the chasm, and tried to get my heart beating again. I could hear Jake freaking out.

"I'm okay, I'm okay," I called out, once I could breathe again.

I pulled up the wire to find nothing but a severed, frayed end. The force of the blast, or maybe shrapnel rock from the seam, must have damaged it.

"How are we going to get the bag across now?" Jake asked.

I shook my head slowly. The obvious answer was for him to toss it across. But given how that had gone with the fruit roll-up, I didn't really like that option. Plus, I had been a much bigger target when I was dangling in front of the vent. Now, the target was basically just the size of the small, rectangular opening itself. And the bag was a lot heavier and more awkward than the fruit roll-ups. Plus the antidote was still in there. It was too much of a risk to have him try to throw.

I held up the glow stick, which now had deep teeth marks in it, and looked around inside the air duct. For as far as I could see ahead of me, it was a straight shot going deeper inside the mountain. Perfectly straight.

Which gave me an idea.

"Jake, find the laser sight and the cutting tool," I called down to him.

He looked at me, both of our faces glowing green in

the light of two glow sticks.

"Hurry!" I said, knowing we likely only had a handful of minutes left before Agent Nineteen's time was up.

His head disappeared into the vent as he searched inside the bag. It reappeared a few moments later, looking determined.

"Which one first?" he asked.

"The laser sight," I said, holding out my cupped hands.

He took a few deep breaths and then tossed it toward me. It was his best attempt yet, but it still wasn't great. It flew just to the right of the opening and although I was able to get a hand on it, it was just the tips of my fingers. The device slipped through them, hit the wall, and then bounced down into the darkness.

If Gollum was living somewhere down there, he was getting a bunch of precious treasures today. Happy birthday, Gollum.

Jake cursed loudly. The word echoed several times up and down the enclosed crevasse.

"It's okay—that was a good practice throw," I said. I knew scolding him would only make him more nervous. I needed to try to ease his mind a little, get him to relax. "That one wasn't the important one anyway."

He nodded.

"Try again. Second time's the charm, right?"

He nodded and extended the laser cutter out of the vent. I held out my hands, trying to give him a good target.

"If you're going to miss, miss too long, not too short," I said. "At least give me a chance."

He nodded one last time and then let it fly. The laser cutter flew right at me, at my face to be precise, much faster than I expected. That, coupled with the weird depth perception the green lighting provided, caused me to flinch. I missed the laser cutter and didn't catch it. Instead, it hit me right in the face as I ducked back into the vent. Thankfully, it was a glancing blow that didn't hurt too badly. It bounced off my face and then slid back into the air duct behind me.

I pounced on it and gripped it as if I would never let go.

"What a throw!" I yelled out toward Jake. I crawled over and gave him a thumbs-up.

He grinned back. "Just call me Joe Blanton."

"Who?" I asked.

"Never mind, just get to work."

I nodded and turned back into the vent. It was hard to know just how long of a section to cut without the laser sight, but I figured cutting too much could be remedied, too little could not. So when I started cutting out the ceiling of the air duct, I went down what I thought was at least twenty feet. Once again, the laser cut through the metal like a lightsaber.

In less than a minute, I had in my hands a long strip of the air duct's ceiling. I was a little concerned about the solid rock behind the vent caving in on me, but to my surprise there was not solid rock behind the strip but a series of pipes and wires running the length of the air duct encased within a larger concrete housing.

I shifted the long strip of air duct metal so it was under me and then began pushing it toward the edge of the vent. I shoved it out into the chasm, careful to keep all my weight on the end so it wouldn't fall. Jake must have figured out right away what I was up to, because when I got near enough to the edge to see him, he was reaching out to receive the other end of the metal strip.

It bowed and bent as more of it was pushed out over the gap. But that actually helped, as it dipped down toward Jake's hands. Finally, he was able to grab the end and then pull it into his vent. There was still a decent length of it left inside my air duct and so I pushed it out a few more feet, then sat on the end to anchor it. It was more difficult to keep it down as the metal strained under the pressure of being bent across a fifteen-foot gap.

"Do you think it will hold?" Jake asked.

"I've got this end anchored. Are there at least five or six feet in there on your end?"

He nodded. "It feels flimsy."

I knew it was a lot to ask him to test it. And more than that, even if it did hold him, it was still just a few feet wide at most, so it would likely be a terrifying crawl across the space. That said, the sheet metal was actually thicker than I'd imagined and I didn't think it was possible for it to break, even with one hundred pounds of middle schooler crawling across it.

"If you don't want to try . . . ," I started.

"No, no, we have to get this across." He held up the bag. "I'll do it."

I had to hand it to him. I had done stuff like this before, so even though I was terrified, I knew how to deal with my fright. This was his first time.

He slung the bag over his shoulder and then took a few seconds, clearly trying to psych himself up. He started with a very tentative first hand, pressing down on the metal with his upper body weight. It hardly budged, which was a good sign. I think it gave him confidence as well, because before I knew it, Jake was crawling across and up the thin metal strip on his hands and knees. After a few feet the metal did bow a little bit and it almost lifted me up, but I shifted so that more of my weight was on the end.

He started slow, but then moved faster once he hit the halfway point. He was almost moving too fast, clearly motivated by terror. But then he was suddenly close enough for me to reach out and grab his hand. I leaned back and pulled him the rest of the way.

Once inside the vent, he sat down with his eyes wide and breathed hard.

"That. Was. Horrifying," he said slowly.

"You're a hero, man," I said, genuinely meaning it.

"It was your idea."

"What can I say," I said with a grin. "I guess we just make a good team."

CHAPTER 25

THE TAPPING OF TIME

A SHORT TIME LATER, AIDED BY THE BLUEPRINTS AND OUR fading glow sticks, we arrived at a five-way junction in the air duct, which I knew meant we were getting close to where the duct emptied into the base.

I shined my green light on the map. It took me a little while to get my bearings. But once I figured out where we were on the map, the next challenge was figuring out which branch to take.

I could almost feel the time ticking away, like some sort of creepy finger tapping on my shoulder in rhythm with my pounding heart. I just needed to calm down and focus. Jake hovering over my shoulder wasn't helping any.

"Do you mind backing off a little bit?" I said, sounding more irritated than I intended, especially considering what we'd already been through together.

"Sorry," he mumbled.

"We need to go this way." I pointed to my left.

"Are you sure?" he said. "I'm pretty sure we need to take the right one."

"Why do you think that?" I asked.

"Because, look, it connects to this vent section which goes right into this hallway. Which leads to this room with the red X on it. I'm assuming that's where we're going, right?"

I tried to follow his finger as he talked, wiping at the sweat dripping into my eyes, frustrated with my own stupidity.

"Are you sure?" I asked. "Lives depend on this."

"Yes, I'm sure," he said, pushing past me. "Come on."

He crawled through the right vent branch. I took one last look at the blueprints. Jake was right. Agent Nineteen was one stupid mistake away from dying, and I almost made that mistake, while Jake had just saved his life for possibly the seventeenth time that day.

I followed him down the vent. A short time later, he held his glow stick over a vent cover under us. We checked the schematic again.

"We're here," he said.

This vent cover had screws on the inside. I used a small screwdriver that Agent Blue had included in my supplies to remove them. The slatted metal clattered to the floor below us. Whatever room we were about to enter was completely dark.

Jake got in position to jump down, but I stopped him. I remembered the small gas mask inside the bag. There was only one of them. It might be kind of awkward to put it on and expect Jake to go without one. Then again, I certainly didn't want to get infected with the fatal Romero Virus, which would cause my brain to literally eat itself.

Agent Blue and Director Isadoris had told me a few days before that the virus should no longer be airborne. The only real risk would be contact with infected people. So if we found any, what would I do?

I searched my backpack of supplies desperately. I still had the extendable rod, the grappling hook harness and a section of the wiring, the laser cutter, the mission-brief documents, the one working gas mask, and the metal box containing the antidote.

I handed the real mask to Jake.

"Put this on," I said.

His eyes widened. "What about you?"

"Don't worry, I have a plan."

I grabbed the laser cutter, the leftover grappling hook wire, and the harness and got to work. First, I took off my jacket and sweatshirt and then tore off the sleeve of the sweatshirt. I cut it down into a double-layered patch big enough to cover my nose and mouth. Then I cut the grappling wire into smaller sections and ran the frayed ends through holes I burned into either end of the patch of sleeve. I did the same to the harness straps, measuring them around my head to make sure I got the size right. In the end, I had a crude makeshift mask of double-layered fleece, bound by wires and secured to my head with chunks of the grappling harness.

It wasn't much, but it had to be better than nothing. The fact that I could barely breathe with it covering half my face had to be a good sign that the virus would have a tough time getting in. And if I somehow did get infected, it's not as if the disease were incurable. I had extra vials of the antidote in my pack.

Jake gave me a wary look, but I shook my head. We didn't have any time left to argue.

"Lower me down?" he suggested, his voice muffled by the mask. "Then when you jump, I'll break your fall. You went first last time."

"Are you sure?"

"Yeah," he said. "It's only fair that I go first this time."

I was starting to like his attitude. He made a good counterpart. Maybe I'd found my own partner? Like how Agent Nineteen had Agent Blue? If Jake continued to prove himself, he might even get to sign on with the Agency as well. And then maybe Isadoris and Blue wouldn't be so mad that I'd broken my cover.

I lowered Jake down as best I could, but he was heavy and I let go a little early. He landed with a thud.

"Sorry," I said.

"It's okay," he said. I could just barely see him standing under the vent opening. "I'm ready."

I tossed down my bag first. He caught it and set it aside. Then he reached up for me as I lowered myself down. He grabbed my legs and held them steady.

"Let go," he said.

I did and he buckled under my weight. We both hit the floor with matching grunts.

And just like that, we had officially infiltrated the secret Agency base inside Teddy Roosevelt's head.

0101010101010100001010100101010100101010100
10101000010010100101010010101010101010101
00001010101010101001100
00101011010100010010
101010000100101001011
001001000001010101001100
101010
01001
0101
1010

CHAPTER 26

BEING TEDDY ROOSEVELT

WE JUST LAY THERE FOR A FEW MOMENTS, CATCHING OUR breath. Then I rolled to the side and climbed to my feet. I took my nearly dead glow stick and shined it around. We were in a hallway not unlike those at the Agency HQ under our school.

Jake got to his feet and rubbed his back.

"Where are those blueprints?" he asked, his voice muffled by the gas mask.

We checked them together.

"We should be right here." He pointed at a hallway

not far from the lab.

"Then we need to go this way," I said, pointing down the hall behind us.

Jake nodded, and we didn't waste any more time getting started toward the Jarmusch Research Lab.

As we jogged down the hallway, I tried to keep my mind from wandering to what we might find. A room full of corpses? A completely empty lab, but one filled with a deadly virus vapor? I didn't know, and thinking about it was only making things worse. So instead I just tried to focus on not letting my jellylike legs collapse on me.

There weren't any dead bodies or signs of a struggle within the base hallways. Which meant two things were becoming increasingly likely:

1. The outbreak was an accident and not the result of enemy infiltration.
2. The base personnel were still alive in quarantine somewhere.

But we would know for sure soon enough. Jake followed me to the right, around a corner, and then suddenly we were there. A lone door stood in front of us. A small label next to it on the wall read:

THE JARMUSCH MICROBIOCHEMISTRY
DEVELOPMENT AND TESTING LABORATORY

"What now?" Jake asked.

I pulled the mission documents from my bag. I didn't know how much time we had left, but it couldn't have been more than a few minutes.

"The base emergency override system is engaged, so a simple passcode should get us in, rather than a retina or fingerprint scan. Supposedly." I pulled out Agent Blue's written instructions with the passcode on it. "I guess."

I typed the nine-digit code into the computer keypad next to the door. As soon as I pressed the first button, the keypad lit up a faint green color. At least Agent Blue had been right about the emergency power still working even after I took out the base's power grid.

After I typed in the code, nothing happened for a few seconds. Then there was a soft click as the door unlocked. I glanced at Jake, who made a motion for me to hurry. I grabbed the door and pulled it open.

The lab was not pitch-black, which was good, because my glow stick was now officially dead. The room was dimly lit by two sets of emergency lights in the corners. It was dark, but there was just enough light to make out everything, kind of like in this fancy restaurant that we went to one time for my dad's birthday.

"Carson, look," Jake said, pointing across the room.

In the far corner was a smaller enclosed area. Behind the glass walls were all sorts of beakers, tubes, high-tech machines, and other expensive-looking lab equipment, in addition to a large walk-in fridge.

Also behind the glass wall was Agent Nineteen.

He was lying on the floor and not moving.

That's when I knew that we were too late.

CHAPTER 27

COUNTDOWN ZERO

THE ONLY THING THAT KEPT ME FROM JUST COLLAPSING TO THE floor in a big heaping pile of failure was the fact that there was another guy behind the glass wall with Agent Nineteen. He was wearing a white lab coat.

And he was very much alive.

The guy waved at us frantically, shouting something. I couldn't hear his voice at all, which was probably to be expected considering he was inside some sort of sealed-off room.

"Come on, we've got to help him!" Jake said as he

rushed over to the smaller glass room within the larger room.

"Wait, we don't . . . ," I started, but then just followed him.

It's not like my sole mission was to save Agent Nineteen. Even if he was already dead, that didn't mean I couldn't still save any of the other Agency personnel who were still alive. But something odd occurred to me as I ran after Jake: Where was everyone else? The only ones behind the glass were Agent Nineteen and the guy in the lab coat. Agent Blue had said there were usually ten agents and staff within the base at any given time. Which meant there should have been eight more people here. Where were they?

When we got to the glass wall and I saw the guy in the lab coat up close, I realized how dire the situation was. He looked like a walking corpse. Animated death. A chunk of rotting cow fat molded into a human being. His eyes were sunken inside baggy yellow sockets and his skin had the color and texture of cake frosting. Sweating cake frosting.

He hit a switch on a steel beam in the middle of the glass wall.

"Thank goodness you're here!" His voice came out through a small intercom speaker sounding as desperate as he looked. "You need to go call for help!"

"We are the help," I said as calmly as I could.

"What do you mean?" the guy said, confusion clearly visible behind his panic.

"The Agency sent us," I said.

"You have the antidote?"

I nodded. Then I pointed at Agent Nineteen, still crumpled on the floor, not moving. I couldn't really see his face to know if he was conscious, alive, zombiefied, or just sleeping. "Is he dead?" I somehow managed to ask without my voice breaking.

Apparently the guy could hear me through the intercom as well because he started shaking his head right away, and there was no way he was reading my lips since they were covered with my makeshift gas mask. And I thought for a very brief moment that it was his way of telling me that Agent Nineteen hadn't made it. But then he spoke again.

"Not yet, but he will be. We both will be, very soon. No more questions, just do exactly as I say, got it?"

I nodded, already taking my backpack off.

"Where is the antidote?" he asked.

I fished out the small, unmarked metal container, the size of a paperback book, and held it up. Relief flooded his empty eyes.

"Over here." He motioned and started walking. As I followed him, I noticed the small steel door on the far side of the glass wall. It was the size of an oven door with a smooth curved handle.

The man hit another intercom switch above the door on his side of the glass.

"Open the door," he said.

"Won't that let the virus out?" I asked.

He shook his head, scowling. "Agent Nineteen and I have mere moments left. It's no longer airborne. But even still, this compartment is airtight, like an air lock in a spaceship in a sci-fi movie. Open the door, now."

I flung it open and put the box inside and then closed it without waiting for his instructions to do so. It's not like I needed to be a scientist to figure that part out.

The guy in the lab coat hit a button. A green light flashed above the door. He opened the compartment from his side and grabbed the box hastily with shaking hands that grew steadier as he opened it and held up one of the glass vials.

"What about Nineteen?" I shouted.

He shook his head, clearly too annoyed to respond to me. But it made sense for him to administer it to himself first. It was like on airplanes, how they always said to secure your own oxygen mask before helping others. If he died in that extra time while trying to get to Nineteen, then they'd both be goners.

His lab coat had a small name tag on it: *Phil*.

Phil removed an injection gun from the case and loaded one of the glass vials into it. Then he pressed it to his neck and shot the liquid into his artery. He breathed in heavily as he did so.

"Phil," I said.

He looked up quickly.

"Now him." I pointed back over to where Agent Nineteen lay motionless.

Phil nodded and hurried to Agent Nineteen's unconscious body. I followed him back over and pressed my face up to the glass. I just hoped it wasn't already too late.

Agent Nineteen didn't move, and I couldn't tell if he was breathing as Phil replaced the needle and antidote vial in the injection gun. His hands moved faster now than they had before. Could the cure be working that quickly? I prayed it could.

He pressed the gun to Agent Nineteen's neck and pulled the trigger. He checked Nineteen's pulse by putting his fingers on his neck and stood up slowly a few seconds later.

"Is he still alive?" I asked.

"His heart rate is low, but still beating," he said.

"When will he wake up?"

Phil shook his head and then frowned. "It's hard to say. It could be a few minutes. A few hours. I really don't know. We haven't yet done human testing of the virus to this stage of progression."

I nodded but allowed myself to breathe a sigh of relief anyway. He wasn't dead. I got here in time to save him. The mission was a success.

"Where is everyone else?" I asked. "How do I get you guys out of there? If it's not airborne anymore, why are you still locked in there? How did the virus even get out for that matter?"

The questions that had built up in my brain like a flooding river suddenly burst through the dam all at once. But before Phil had a chance to say anything, Jake spoke up.

"Whoa! Mr. Jensen from school is the guy you were sent to save?"

I clearly had a lot more to explain. But my head was still reeling. I felt like I might pass out. The makeshift gas mask I was wearing certainly wasn't helping.

"You can take off your masks," Phil said, reading my mind. "I assure you, whatever quantities of the virus that were airborne within the base have long since died. As for your questions, I'll get to those in a little bit, but first I have some questions of my own for you. Then we'll work on getting us all out of here safely."

He was clearly the ranking Agency official in this situation, so I wasn't about to argue. Besides, I was way too exhausted for that.

"You say the Agency sent you in," Phil said. "But you're just kids."

I explained to him the reasons the Agency chose me for this mission, staying vague when explaining that I'd done some freelance work for the Agency earlier that year. I assumed that if he needed to know about my Olek mission, he probably already would. Then I told him how Jake had followed me and saved me when I'd fallen, hastily defending my decision to let him continue on the mission with me.

Phil nodded slowly as I talked. "Who actually sent you?" he asked.

"Director Isadoris and Agent Blue," I said.

"Remarkable," he said again. "Well, you did a fine job, young man."

"Zero," I said. "You can call me Agent Zero."

"Okay, then, Agent Zero," Phil said, checking his wristwatch. "Let's get to your questions, then we'll go about getting us all out of here. Fire away."

I thought back to my string of questions. There were so many of them.

"Where is everybody else?" I asked.

"I'm afraid they didn't make it," Phil said somberly.

"Really?" I asked, an emptiness taking the place of my stomach. "But how?"

"They were sealed off in another part of the base when the outbreak occurred. In the panic that followed, there was a small explosion in that sector that both destroyed and collapsed the emergency ventilation system, and, well, I don't want to get into grisly details, but let me assure you that they didn't suffer. Thankfully there were only seven staff on duty when the outbreak occurred, so casualties could have been worse. Not that that diminishes the loss of some very dear friends and colleagues."

As he said this, he seemed to sink a few inches lower to the ground if that were possible. He just looked so haggard and defeated. I realized that to me this had been a stressful yet successful mission, and to him it had to have been one of the worst experiences of his life. He'd just lost a bunch of coworkers and pals and almost died himself. If I lost seven of my friends in one day, I'd basically be completely alone.

"How did the virus get out?" I asked.

"It was simply a mistake. A very tragic and horrendous mistake, which is what has made this all particularly hard to stomach. Even the most highly trained scientists are prone to errors from time to time . . ." He trailed off, checking his watch again.

Did he have somewhere to be? Or was it a force of habit? I guess most of the science teachers I'd ever known in my life were the kind of people who had never been late for anything in their lives.

"You said earlier that the virus wasn't airborne anymore," I said. "If that's the case, then why are you two still locked in there?"

"Once there's a contamination, the system will automatically seal the lab and the Red Room, which is what we call this glass case you see here. It cannot be overridden from the inside. Unfortunately, there was nobody left to manually open it for us once we were able to contain what was left of the virus and its potency period wore off. That said, would you mind if I talked you through the release procedures so we can get Agent Nineteen a medevac? I'm concerned that he hasn't yet regained consciousness."

I nodded.

"Okay, I'm assuming they wouldn't send you in here without the quarantine override code," Phil said. "It changes every twelve hours automatically and can only be accessed in Agency terminals outside the base itself. A panic fail-safe of sorts."

"Yeah, I have it memorized," I said, trying to recall it. I hadn't thought about the code since earlier that morning.

"Good," Phil said, looking relieved. He walked me through a number of steps needed to release the emergency quarantine seal on the Red Room.

Eventually we got to the last step, which was to input the code into a computer monitor nearby. As soon as I put my mind to it, I remembered it almost instantly. I typed it in and the door to the glass room clicked open.

I rushed inside and knelt next to Agent Nineteen. There was dried blood on his head, and he looked pretty much like any dead body I'd seen in movies. But he was breathing, so that was a good sign. I looked up again to ask Phil how we were going to carry him out.

That's when I found myself face-to-face with the business end of a handgun.

"¿Cómo está?" the gun seemed to say. *"Mi nombre es La Pistola, y estas a punto de morir."*

For some reason, in my head, the gun spoke Spanish.

910101010101010000101001010101001010101001010
1010100001001010010101010010101010101010101
9000100011001100101010101010101010
901000010101010100101010101001
1010100101010101010101
100010101010101010

CHAPTER 28

LA PISTOLA

IGNORED THE GUN'S COMMENTS AND LOOKED PAST IT WHILE MY brain attempted to catch up with what my eyes were showing me. The first thing I saw was Jake, emerging from a huge walk-in fridge within the Red Room.

"I got it," Jake called out, holding something in his hands.

His voice sounded distant, like this was all happening underwater. What did he have? Why was he telling me? Furthermore, did he not see La Pistola pointed at me?

I tried to yell out for him to run. That it wasn't safe

in here after all. But instead all I could think about was the gun.

I finally focused on the person holding it. Phil pointed it at me steadily as a smile stretched across his lips.

"What's going on?" I asked.

"It doesn't matter," he said before checking his watch again. "All that matters is that you don't move. Do exactly as I say, and neither of you will get hurt."

Jake stood next to Phil, holding several metal containers similar to the one that had held the antidote. He held them up.

"Got them," Jake said, still not looking at me.

Phil examined both containers briefly, and for a split second I debated making a move to disarm him while he was distracted. But who was I kidding? He was a good six feet away from me. I'd have to move faster than was humanly possible to cover the distance before he noticed and pulled the trigger.

"Jake, what's going on?" I asked.

Finally, Jake looked at me. Then he smiled. But not his normal smile. This smile was twisted and sick, like a circus clown's smile. It was the sort of expression that gave little kids nightmares for years. It was the kind of look that people needed therapy to deal with.

"You . . . who are you?" I asked weakly.

Jake didn't even bother responding. Instead he looked up at Phil again and asked, "How much time do we have?"

"Plenty," Phil said. "But let's not take any chances. Come on."

He motioned toward the door, and he and Jake both stepped out of the room and resealed it from the outside. They stood there, on the other side of the glass wall, and grinned at me with shockingly similar smiles. I glanced again at the metal containers in Jake's hands and suddenly had a feeling that I knew precisely what they contained.

This was bad.

Very bad.

Understatement of the year, Carson. No, better make that the century. How about ever, in the history of the universe? Yeah, that was probably most correct.

I watched them turn to leave without offering me any explanations or answers or clues as to what was going on. The door shut behind them, and we were alone.

ZERO TIMES ZERO
EQUALS ZERO

I DIDN'T REALLY KNOW WHAT TO DO, SO I JUST SAT IN ONE OF THE
chairs by the nearest lab table and put my face in my
hands. I had a million questions, but was concentrating
on the one fact that mattered most right now: I was alive.
Agent Nineteen and I were both alive.

But why? If Phil was some sort of enemy agent, why
give Agent Nineteen the antidote at all?

The answer hit me just as quickly: to gain my trust.
He did it so I would let him out of the sealed room, since
I was the only one with the quarantine-override code.

Which I'd given him, letting him out into the open having stolen not only what was left of the antidote but also—if I was right about what was in those cases Jake had taken—an apocalyptic virus that could usher in the end of modern civilization in less than a month.

I shook my head slowly from side to side as if that could somehow undo all this.

Twice.

That was twice now that I'd thought I was helping to save the world, yet was unwittingly assisting some master villain with a diabolical scheme. And it was partly because I'd broken my primary directive as an agent: Keep Your Cover at All Costs. I'd gone ahead and broken the rule by bringing Jake in and now the mission had gone from bad to terrible.

Jake. Jake was an enemy agent, too. How could I have been so stupid? I was like a Bad Guy Secret Weapon. A double agent who didn't even know he was a double agent. I couldn't even be a proper single agent.

Agent Zero was sort of a fitting name for me, if you really thought about it.

A few minutes later, Agent Nineteen finally stirred. It started with a light groan, and then he opened his eyes and sat up. He rubbed his head where dried blood had matted his hair and then winced immediately.

"Agent Nineteen, you're awake!" I said, stating the obvious like the idiot that I was.

He looked at me groggily, trying to get his bearings.

"What time is class?" he asked. "Are you late again, Carson?"

I would have laughed were we not trapped inside a secret government lab. Especially because I was never late to music class. It was the one class I was actually mostly on time for. Well, now that I'd signed that contract with Gomez, I would never be late to any classes again.

Then I almost started to cry when I realized that I didn't even know if I'd ever get back to Minnow at all. But Agent Nineteen suddenly waking up gave me at least a little hope. This was what he did—he saved the day. He was a real hero.

He was the anti–Agent Zero. He was at least Nineteen better than Zero.

"What's funny?" he asked, then rubbed his eyes and looked around.

"Nothing," I said.

Which was true. I'd laughed, but it had been one of those moments where you laugh because what you're thinking about is so depressing that laughing is all you can do to keep from crying.

"Carson, what are you doing here?" he asked, seeming to get a sense of where he was. "Wait. If you're in here . . ."

His eyes went wide and he climbed to his feet. He moved slower than usual, but still a lot faster than I would have expected considering how dead he had looked just a few minutes ago. He wobbled once he was on his feet but steadied himself on a nearby table. Then he looked around.

After seeing nothing but an empty, mostly dark lab, his eyes drifted back to me. When I saw his face, it was enough to make the panic return in full force, like a double-barreled Super Soaker filled with corrosive acid blasting me in the torso at point-blank range.

"He got out?" Agent Nineteen asked.

"You mean Phil?"

Agent Nineteen slammed his hand onto the metal table. It was scary seeing a teacher lose control and act out so violently, even if we weren't at school and even if he wasn't really a teacher. The sound was almost like a gunshot inside the sealed room.

Agent Nineteen gave me that desperately hopeless look again. The one that melted my vital organs instantaneously.

"Did he get the virus?" he asked.

"Was it in a small metal box in that fridge over there?" I asked, my voice shaking, as I pointed across the room to the door I'd seen Jake come out of.

Then Agent Nineteen did something that I really didn't expect. Something that almost terrified me more than anything else that had happened to me that day. He picked up the stool he'd been sitting on and threw it across the lab with incredible force while letting out a scream of pure rage.

The stool slammed into the glass wall of the Red Room, bounced off it, and crashed into some lab equipment on a nearby table. The beakers and vials shattered and smashed to the floor as the stool slid across the table and eventually came to a stop in a large metal sink.

I took two steps back and cowered, fearing that he might come after me next. I was the one who had let Phil get away with the virus, after all. I had been responsible for this.

But Agent Nineteen regained control again, and instead of coming after me, he simply slumped down onto the floor in a sitting position. He looked at me, his eyes watering, close to tears. I didn't think I could handle seeing a teacher violently freak out and cry within one minute of each other.

He didn't cry though. Instead, he just sat there and shook his head.

So I did the same. I sat down on the ground and tried to pretend I wasn't as scared as I was. Because if I let myself buy in to what I was feeling, I'd definitely start bawling. If there was anything I could do about it, I would die with at least a little bit of my dignity left. Whatever dignity could be left after breaking an unbreakable rule that had helped lead to an apocalyptic virus falling into enemy hands.

"Can't we go stop them?" I asked. "Aren't you even going to try?"

He just stared straight ahead. "The door can't be opened from the inside when the lab is under quarantine. There is no override I can activate from in here."

"Won't the Agency send someone else?"

"No—for the same reasons, I imagine, that they sent you in here, rather than sending another agent. But even if they were going to send another strike team, it wouldn't do any good. We're both going to be dead in . . ."

He checked his watch.

"Twenty-two minutes."

01010101010100001010010101010010101010100
10101000010010100101010100101010101010101
00001   0011001010101010101010
0010   001010101001010101001
101   1010100101010101010101
                110010101010101010101

CHAPTER 30

ANOTHER COUNTDOWN

"**W**HAT? WHY?" I SHOUTED. ANOTHER TICKING CLOCK? I was getting tired of countdowns that would end with the death of someone close to me. Which, in this case, was me.

"The Base Security Breach Self-Destruct Sequence has been initiated. The BSBSDS, as we call it. Or sometimes we just call it the Proverbial Fan."

"But who would do that?" I asked. "Was it Phil? Did he initiate the self-destruction?"

"No, it was me," Agent Nineteen said.

"But—" I started. Agent Nineteen interrupted my feeble attempt to grasp the situation.

"I locked us in here," he said. "I initiated the self-destruct. I was trying to keep Phil from getting his hands on the virus and escaping. And I'd succeeded . . ."

He didn't need to finish his thought. He'd succeeded until I had shown up and ruined it. Not that I'd really known what I was doing. And I'm sure he knew that. But it didn't matter. Telling me it was my fault couldn't make me feel any worse than I already did.

"But that means you would have died," I said.

"Yes. Some things are more important than one agent's life. Do I want to die? Of course not. But if that's what it takes to keep the virus from falling into the wrong hands, then so be it."

"Can't you contact the Agency? Override the system? Stop the self-destruct?"

Agent Nineteen shook his head slowly from side to side.

"It's inevitable now," he said calmly, as if he were talking about Johann Sebastian Bach's final opus in class. "It cannot be stopped. Not by anyone. Not even Director Isadoris. This base will explode in nineteen minutes. Or, I should say, it will implode. This base was designed so that the implosion will destroy the base from the inside, cushioning the exterior of the mountain from the transferred energy of the blast. So Roosevelt's face will survive. Nobody outside will know that anything happened. It's an ingenious design, a completely new theory of energy transferal formulated by one of the Agency's top demolition engineers."

"The Agency won't even know it imploded?"

"Oh, no. Right before implosion, the system will transmit all the base's encrypted data via a secure Agency radio frequency. They'll know everything that happened in here . . . after it's all over."

"Why would it only transmit later?"

"It's a security measure," he said. "To make sure that whatever breach happened here stays here. Although, I suppose, in this particular case it backfired. They sent you in, after all. But I imagine that likely had something to do with Phil cutting off the normal lines of communication before he released the virus, rather than a failure of our protocol."

"So who is Phil? How did he even get in here?"

"He was one of our most trusted research-and-development agents. Science Officer Ichabod was his official Agency codename. Although he always preferred to just be called Phil. He's worked for the Agency for over ten years, developing advanced biochemical weaponry and disaster prevention. It was a shock to those of us here when he sabotaged his own project and executed his plan. And while I still don't know why he did it, I suspect it may link back to Medlock, somehow."

I sighed. There wasn't much else to say. We both just sat there thinking about stuff. I had no idea what Agent Nineteen was thinking, but I was thinking about my family and friends. How I'd never see them again. How they'd probably never find out how I really died. It made me wonder what sort of story the Agency would spin and how they'd manage to feed it to the school and public. After a while, it was just too much to think about.

And then I finally did start to cry. Agent Nineteen didn't say anything or try to comfort me. He just let me sit there and cry in peace.

0101010101010000101001010100101010100
10101000010010100101010100101010101010101
00001   0011001010101010101010
0010   0010101010010101010100
101   10101001010101010101
000   110010101010101010

CHAPTER 31

THE FORTY-THIRD
STREET SAINT

EVENTUALLY MY WELL OF TEARS RAN DRY. I WIPED AT MY RED eyes with no shame. Who would blame me for crying? Knowing your death is imminent is indescribably horrible, and I wouldn't even wish it upon Phil, the evil psycho who had done this to us.

"How long?" I asked.

Agent Nineteen checked his watch slowly, like a person with all the time in the world to spare.

"Nine minutes," he said.

"Oh."

I wasn't sure what else to say. What was an appropriate response to someone calmly informing you that you had nine minutes left to live? But after a few more seconds of silence, I finally did think of something else to say.

"So, how did you end up becoming an agent, anyway?"

"It's a good question," he said, nodding slowly. "Most of our agents are recruited internally via intel we have on other US agencies like the FBI, CIA, military special ops, Navy Seals, et cetera. But a handful of agents, including me, are recruited in more unique ways. Situations like yours, for instance."

"So you became a secret agent by accident, too?" I said.

Nineteen nodded. "That's one way to put it," he said. "About twelve years ago, a bridge collapsed in my hometown. Almost thirty people died. I happened to have been riding my bike across the bridge that day. I was twenty years old at that time, going to college to be a psychologist. When the middle section of the bridge gave way, the whole thing shook and I was thrown from my bike and momentarily knocked unconscious. It was when I was finally able to get up, collect myself, and realize what was going on that I noticed the school bus.

"It was dangling on the edge of the collapsed bridge. There were screams everywhere, but the only ones I could hear were those of the kids inside the bus. I hardly remember what happened next. I wasn't even thinking at that point, I just knew that *someone* had to do *something*."

"Wait—was this that bridge collapse that happened in Spirit Falls?" I asked.

"I'm surprised you know about that. You were, what, two years old?"

"Ms. Lee gave us this reading assignment last year where we read a bunch of articles in old magazines and newspapers about 'unsung heroes.' The Spirit Falls incident was on the front page of one of the magazines. So . . . you're the Forty-Third Street Saint?"

Agent Nineteen nodded. "Yes. That was me."

"No one knew who you were! Most people thought you died after you got the kids out and the bus finally fell into the river! Why didn't you ever come forward? You're a hero."

"Because I didn't do it to be a hero. I don't even know why I did it. I just heard those screams and acted. It's as simple as that. To me, knowing the kids all survived was what mattered. If I had realized what I was doing, or stopped to think it over, I probably wouldn't have acted at all. And those kids would be dead."

"So what happened next?"

"The Agency was able to track me down. At the time, I had no idea how they did it, but one day I get home from school and there are two agents waiting there for me. The Agency has a whole department whose sole function is recruitment. We call them the Talent Scouts. They monitor CIA operations, FBI stings, military engagements, and also everyday occurrences like the bridge collapse. They identify individuals who display certain qualities and behaviors in extreme circumstances. For instance, one of our agents is a former World Series of Poker Champion, and another was recruited through a reality TV show for being able to withstand hours of 'torture' while simultaneously computing complex math problems in his head.

"Even after that, though, only a very small percentage of the people scouted end up becoming agents. There is a rigorous vetting process that weeds out over ninety-eight percent of possible candidates. It's not even until the last few tests that the recruits even know what they're getting involved with. There are psych exams, extensive background checks, all sorts of procedures and tests."

"Wow," I said.

"Yes," he agreed.

"Did you know that Jake was in on this somehow?" I said.

"Jake Tyson-Gulley?" Agent Nineteen asked like that couldn't actually be true.

Then it dawned on me that Agent Nineteen had been unconscious that whole time. He had no idea that Jake was somehow working for the enemy. And I hadn't told him yet, because I'd been way too distracted by the fact that we were going to get crushed inside an imploding secret base soon.

"Yeah, turns out Jake is an enemy agent. Who knew, right?" I said. "He saved me when I was climbing up here and then I had to tell him about the mission. I needed his help to get in anyway."

Agent Nineteen shook his head with an expression on his face that was clearly a mixture of disbelief and disappointment.

"I know I shouldn't have broken my cover," I said. "I'm sorry."

"You're right," Agent Nineteen said. "You shouldn't have. But that doesn't really matter anymore, does it?"

I shrugged.

"Unbelievable," Agent Nineteen muttered to himself.

"Medlock somehow infiltrated the schools."

"Yeah, he and Phil seemed to know each other and he helped him get the virus," I said, trying to keep the focus off what I'd done. "If you used a kid then why is it so shocking that the enemy could use them as well?"

"We only used you because Medlock's plan forced our hand. He involved you directly on purpose and we unwittingly played into that," Agent Nineteen said with surprisingly humble honesty. "Then again, it was probably naive of us to assume he wouldn't try to recruit his own inside agent eventually."

I looked at my feet, picking at the little rocks caught in the soles of my shoes. My eyes burned as if they wanted to cry again. But there were no tears left. We only had a few minutes left to live. This was confirmed by the sudden flashing of a red emergency light in the center of the lab's ceiling.

Then a female voice crackled over the intercom.

"Three minutes to facility self-destruction. Please evacuate immediately."

I recognized the voice. It was the same one that had gotten me involved in all this to begin with earlier that year. It was Besty. But if I had been hoping to catch up with her, it clearly wasn't going to happen. She didn't even repeat the warning, as she had with the self-destructing data device I'd brought to school earlier that year. Instead she left us in silence to contemplate our demise.

Agent Nineteen and I locked eyes.

Then suddenly he shifted his gaze to something behind me and a look of pure shock spread across his face.

010101010101010000101001010101001010101010 0
101010000100101001010101001010101010101010101
0000101010101010100011001 101010
0010101101010001001010 1001
10101000010010100101 0101
00001010101010101001110

CHAPTER 32

AWKWARD FRIEND HUGS

I SPUN AROUND, AND GAPED.

On the other side of the glass wall, Danielle peered in at us with a panicked expression on her face.

I jumped up and hit the button on the intercom. "What are you doing here?" I asked.

Dumbest question of the year, I know. What I meant to ask was how in the world she'd gotten inside the base. And furthermore, how she had even known the base was here at all. But instead of clarifying I just stood there and stared in shock.

"There's not really time for stupid questions right now, Carson!" she said. "Didn't you just hear that? We have three minutes, so you guys need to tell me what to do to get you out of there!"

That was Danielle for you. She always was an excellent prioritizer.

Agent Nineteen sprang to his feet behind me.

"Mr. Jensen? What the heck are you doing here?"

"Same answer, Danielle," he said. "Now listen to me very carefully."

He began giving Danielle precise, clear instructions. She put her shock aside immediately and carried them out. I marveled at how well they both acted under pressure. Then again, I sometimes did, too, right?

Danielle located the terminal per the instructions, I gave her the passcode at the end, and just like that we were out of the Glass Cage of Death. I rushed over and gave her a huge hug. I wasn't sure if I'd ever hugged Danielle before, but I didn't care how awkward it was at that moment.

"We're not out of the woods just yet, Carson," Agent Nineteen said, rushing past us. "We only have ninety-six seconds. Follow me!"

And so we followed him as he ran out of the lab. After exerting so much energy scaling the mountainside and then sitting still for almost an hour, my legs were basically goop. I wobbled as I ran, struggling to keep up. Danielle kept grabbing my hand to hurry me along.

I thought we'd be headed to the same vent that Jake and I had entered through, but instead we went a completely different way. We went down a few long hallways, illuminated only by flashing red emergency evacuation lights. Down one of the adjoining halls I swore I glimpsed a dead body. One of the base employees, no doubt. I pretended that my eyes had been playing tricks on me in the hallway of the dark base.

Finally, we reached a room—a small laundry room, of all things. But it made sense if you really thought about it. Secret agents and scientists still had to wash their clothes somehow, didn't they?

"We have twenty-two seconds," Agent Nineteen said, panting as he jumped on top of one of the industrial driers.

He grabbed some pipes in the ceiling and then swung both legs forward and kicked at the aluminum drier vent duct. It ripped away from the ceiling with a screech, revealing a hole clogged with dust and fuzz.

"Let's go!" he said, holding down a hand toward Danielle.

She grabbed it and he hoisted her up in one easy motion. He helped her climb into the vent and then handed her a small flashlight he'd gotten from somewhere. Seriously, seeing Agent Nineteen in action was incredible. He was the real deal. Not a bumbling poser like me.

"You're next, let's go!" he shouted, snapping me out of my daze.

I grabbed his hand and he lifted me atop the dryer and into the vent. I started crawling forward without waiting for further instructions. Danielle was already a good ten feet ahead of me.

Then Agent Nineteen was behind me, pushing at my feet.

"Go, Zero, go," he said. "It's a straight shot, just keep crawling."

It worked. His constant shoving did seem to manifest an extra burst of energy from somewhere inside my exhausted, heaping excuse of a human body. I crawled faster, gaining on Danielle a little at a time. Twenty seconds had surely passed since he'd last said we only had twenty seconds left. Was the self-destruct system faulty? Or had the implosion already begun?

The answer became pretty obvious two seconds later when the metal sides of the vent began caving in with small, crinkling dents. We were surrounded by constant popping noises as little by little, the walls closed in around us. It sounded kind of like popcorn. But much deadlier, obviously, and not nearly as appetizing.

Suddenly there was light in front of us, much more intense than that of Danielle's small flashlight. Before I even realized what was happening, Danielle's outline in front of me disappeared as she exited the vent shaft. The vent walls continued to constrict. So much so that I was nearly crawling on my stomach now.

Agent Nineteen gave me one final hard shove and I went sprawling out of the vent and into the open air. I landed on a pile of brush and pinecones on an incline, and rolled down the hill a short way before managing to catch myself.

I stood up just in time to see Agent Nineteen squeeze himself out of a small opening in the side of the hill. Then suddenly it collapsed on itself, filling with dirt, rocks, and earth. And just like that the vent was gone, as if it had never even existed in the first place.

There was no explosion. No flames. No rumbling boom, or ground-shaking transfer of energy. There was nothing but the outline of a hole on a small hillside in a remote forest. The secret base had simply ceased to exist the way one would expect of a base that nobody knew even existed in the first place.

For a few moments the three of us just stood there under the tall trees and looked at one another with dazed expressions on our faces.

But then suddenly Danielle smiled and jumped up and down in celebration like she'd just found out she'd won a $450 million lottery jackpot. And I suppose that we had just won the lottery, in a sense. Except instead of getting money we got to not get crushed inside a metal tube like pickled fish or something.

And so I joined in the celebration. I hugged Danielle again and we jumped up and down on the hill for a few seconds. Agent Nineteen acted more like an adult, of course, but he also was grinning ear to ear.

His smile quickly faded, and I assumed it was reality settling in. Phil was on the loose, and in possession of one of the most deadly viruses in the history of humankind.

Danielle and I both stopped jumping. I looked at her, only a few inches away, and we separated quickly.

"So," she said, glancing back and forth between Agent Nineteen and me. "Can either of you guys tell me what the heck is going on?"

01010101010101010101001100101010101010101010
010101010101000010100101010010101010100
10101000010010100101010010101010101010101
00001...................001100101010101010101010
0010...................001010101001010101001
101...................101010010101010101
100...................1100101010101010101

CHAPTER 33

VACUUMS AND
APPLEBEE'S DINNERS

AGENT NINETEEN HELPED ME CAREFULLY EXPLAIN THE SITUA-
tion to Danielle. I imagined it was okay to finally break
my cover in this instance since Danielle had just seen
everything firsthand anyway. And it did feel way better
to finally tell my secret with Agency approval. And to tell
an actual friend at that, as opposed to that backstabber
Jake. As she listened, Danielle's face alternated between
shock, fear, and amusement. After seeing what she had
inside the base, I'm guessing there was little that she
wasn't ready to believe.

"So," she finally said, "you've been a . . . secret agent . . . this whole time?"

"Carson can tell you more as we walk," Agent Nineteen said. "We need to head back to the school group. They've no doubt noticed that you're both missing by now. And I need to get in touch with Agent Blue as soon as possible. There's no telling what Phil plans to do with the virus."

Danielle and I followed Agent Nineteen as he walked across and down the hillside toward a stream at the bottom of a shallow valley.

"Before you ask anything," I said to Danielle, "you have to tell me: How in the world did you find us?"

"Yeah, I'd like to know, too," Agent Nineteen said.

"I definitely knew something was up," Danielle said. "Carson has been acting strange lately, for one. But more than that, well . . . I've just never really trusted Jake. There's something about him that has always made me feel uneasy. So when I saw that both of you were gone, and spotted Jake crawling up the hillside, I followed him. I eventually lost sight of him, but it didn't take too long to find footprints leading to the crevice under Roosevelt's face. It was a risk going inside, but I didn't know what else to do. I just had a bad feeling about it all."

"That means you crossed the chasm on the metal plank?" I asked, feeling sick to my stomach thinking about what would have happened if she'd fallen.

Danielle nodded.

"Wow," I said.

"It's truly impressive that you followed them in," Agent Nineteen said, "simply because you were worried about Carson. Did you see Jake and an older gentleman come out of the base on your way up?"

Danielle shook her head, clearly confused by the question. So I explained to her that Jake had been working for the enemy all along.

"I knew something was up with him!" Danielle said. "I knew it."

"You were right all along," I agreed.

Agent Nineteen shook his head slowly, once again having a hard time coming to grips with the fact that a student had been used against the Agency. And then he spent the next twenty-five minutes grilling us for every last bit of information we knew about Jake as we walked.

"I can't believe you told Jake your secret before me," Danielle said once Agent Nineteen seemed to be finished questioning us.

"It's not that I didn't want to tell you," I said. "Jake

caught me red-handed. And saved my life. I didn't know what else to do. Besides, it's because I care about you so much that I didn't want to get you involved in any of this."

"I just can't believe how many lies you told us."

"I know, me either," I said, looking at my feet instead of her face.

After we got to the base of the hill, we followed the creek around it, staying in the shallow valley. Before long, I could once again see the edges of the presidents' stone faces above us at the top of the mountain. All four were still intact. That genius engineer who came up with the physics of an imploding secret base should be rewarded with a Medal of Honor. Or a million bucks. Or something. At least a free dinner at his local Applebee's.

It wasn't much longer before the wooden staircase tourist trail was also in view. There were a few people in park ranger uniforms walking around the base of it as if they were looking for something. Like a couple of missing kids, perhaps.

Agent Nineteen ducked behind a particularly thick tree. Danielle and I did the same without needing to be told.

"Okay, I'll have to leave you here," he said. "But first, Danielle, I need to know that you realize all of this must be kept secret. You can't tell anyone, not your mom or brother, anyone. Understand? In the interests of national security."

Danielle nodded.

"Okay, I trust you can turn yourselves in?" Agent Nineteen said.

We both nodded.

"Good. Just tell them you wandered off by accident and got lost. I'm sure you'll come up with something," he said, directly to me.

"Are you calling me a good liar?" I asked.

"You've earned it," he said.

I truly didn't know if I should be offended or flattered. A little of both, probably.

"What about Phil and Jake?" I asked. "What do we say about Jake?"

"The truth: that you don't know where he went."

I nodded. That seemed simple enough.

"What about Phil?" I asked. "He's still out there."

"Don't worry about that," Agent Nineteen said. "We'll take care of him. Just get yourselves back to the group without arousing any more suspicion."

CHAPTER 34

TROLL HUNTING

SELLING THE LIE WAS EASY ENOUGH. IT HELPED THAT DANIELLE was with me. She'd never been suspected of helping with any of my pranks or getting into any kind of trouble at all, for that matter. So Mr. Gist and Ms. Pearson believed our story about how we'd noticed that Jake had snuck away and we had gone to find him and then gotten lost ourselves.

After that, they went back to working with the park officials to locate Jake. There was no sign of Agent Blue until we got inside the visitor center, where most of the other kids were hanging out. We locked eyes and a faint smile spread across his face. I shook my head slightly to let him know that everything was not exactly okay.

He furrowed his brow but was too busy consoling two melodramatic seventh graders who'd already decided to start crying over Jake being missing. If only they knew why he was gone . . . well, actually, I guess if they knew the truth, they'd probably still be crying, but for a whole different reason.

"Where were you guys?" Dillon asked with a slightly accusatory tone. "And where's Jake?"

I exchanged a quick glance with Danielle and saw in that one look that she knew we couldn't tell him the truth. That she now was beginning to understand my dilemma.

"We don't know," I said.

Danielle and I told him the same story we'd told the park rangers and other chaperones. He didn't believe us, but it honestly would have been a lot more disturbing and out of character if he had.

"You were out searching for Forest Trolls, weren't you?" he said. "I knew it. They're real, and you saw one. Or maybe you saw Smallfoot and didn't tell me because you hate admitting it when I'm right?"

"Come on, Dillon," I said, even though deep down I was so happy to be getting the chance to hear more of his theories after being sure I was about to die just a half hour ago.

"But I do know you've been keeping a secret from me," he said.

"What?" I asked. "How?"

"Because I know what it is," he said. "I know your secret. And I can't believe you told Jake, but not Danielle and me!"

I glanced at Danielle again, not sure what to say. She shook her head, telling me she didn't know how he knew. "Um . . . tell Jake what?"

"Come on, Carson, you know I'd never make you feel bad for needing special toilet paper," he said quietly, trying to keep my secret concealed. "Right?"

I had to bite my lip to keep from letting the relief show on my face. He must have still been awake that night and heard us talking, and then only faked talking in his sleep when we got back.

"Yeah, I should have told you." I nodded like I was ashamed. "He caught me. Otherwise I never would have told him either."

"It's okay," Dillon said. "Jake's a cool guy. I'd trust him with my secrets, too."

"Yeah," I said, "he is a cool guy."

As we all waited for Jake to be found, which I knew he wouldn't be, I made sure to keep an eye on Agent Blue. I was mostly watching him for signals, sure that he'd try to pull me aside to find out what was going on. But he never did. Instead he looked and acted just like you'd expect a teacher chaperone to act in his position, nothing more, nothing less.

But a little while later, as we were all eating Burger King that Ms. Pearson had run into town to get us, I saw Agent Blue calmly look at his phone, say something to Mr. Gist, and then step out of the visitor center quietly.

"I gotta run to the bathroom," I said to Dillon and Danielle.

"What happened to saving the world?" Dillon asked.

I paused. "Huh?"

"Isn't that what you said you call it now?"

"Oh, yeah, but I don't have to do that," I said.

Not waiting to talk about it more, I slipped out the side door, toward the guest restrooms. But I walked right by the men's room and toward the exit door at the end of the hallway. Just as I reached it, a hand grabbed my arm.

"Where are you really going?" Danielle asked.

"Come on," I said, stepping outside.

I figured there was no point in trying to stop her from coming with me. She already knew everything now, anyway. Plus, I owed her one. Well, I actually owed her more like ten hundred thousand billion, or however many favors a life is worth.

She followed me through the exit. Just as we got outside, I caught a glimpse of Agent Blue's jacket ducking behind some trees and heading down a hill toward the large amphitheater adjacent to the west branch of the walking trail.

We started toward the amphitheater and it didn't take long to spot him again, going behind the stage building. We jogged down the concrete steps built into the hillside. When we neared the building, I heard voices and slowed. Danielle and I both walked as softly and quietly as we could toward the corner of the building until the voices were just barely audible.

"Why did you send him after me? Why did you send anyone for that matter?" one of the voices said in a harsh whisper.

I recognized it as Agent Nineteen. Agent Blue responded a little louder, but also in a whisper.

"You'd have done the same for me. Was I just supposed to let you die?"

"Of course you were—it's protocol," Agent Nineteen said. "There was a reason no distress signal was sent. I initiated the self-destruct and the quarantine lockdown. I simply couldn't risk letting Phil get away with the virus. And now it's out. You should have trusted me to have the situation under control."

Agent Blue was silent, but only for a moment. "Director Isadoris had my full support. Nothing about the information transmitted to us indicated that the base had been compromised. We didn't even know if you were still alive."

"That's because *Phil* cut off the emergency transmitter," Agent Nineteen said, "but I suppose that doesn't matter now. The fact is we've got a potential national disaster on our hands. And we need to stop it as soon as possible."

"I've already started prepping the mobile base unit," Agent Blue said. "It's just down the hillside in Keystone."

"I hope it's a four-person MBU," Agent Nineteen said loudly. Too loudly. "Since there will be four of us."

Uh-oh.

I looked at Danielle. She shrugged.

"Yes, we know you're back there," Agent Nineteen said. "You might as well come on out."

Danielle and I rounded the corner and walked over to them.

"Sorry," I said.

"It's okay," said Agent Nineteen. "The fact is that you're involved in this now, whether we like it or not."

"What's she doing here?" Agent Blue asked, pointing at Danielle.

"We have a lot to tell you," Agent Nineteen said. "We can go over it on our way down to the mobile unit."

Agent Blue nodded.

"Don't you need to go back and get us excused or something?" I asked.

"There's no time, we can deal with that mess later," Agent Blue said. "Stopping Phil from releasing that virus is significantly more important than worrying about covering for your absence. There's too much at stake to waste any more time."

0101010101010000101001010100101010101010
1010100001001010010101010010101010101010
00001   00110010101010101010101010
0010   00101010100101010100
101   101010010101010101010
000   11001010101010101010
CHAPTER 35

BLUE IN BROWN
SHORT SHORTS

THE AGENCY'S MOBILE BASE UNIT, OR MBU, WAS DISGUISED AS a UPS truck. It was parked on a side street in a nearby tourist town named Keystone just down the mountainside from Mount Rushmore. The four of us took a small car that Agent Blue broke into and stole from the monument parking ramp.

"It's in the interest of national security," Agent Blue said when Danielle gave him a disapproving look as he started the car using some high-tech key device. "It would take too much time to walk."

Ten minutes later we arrived at the truck, which was parked behind a row of gift shops and restaurants.

The inside of the truck itself looked a lot like Agent Nineteen's secret office at school: high-tech, slick, and expensive. As soon as we entered, the agents disappeared to the front of the truck to get some equipment prepped.

"Wow," Danielle said, looking around, her eyes wide.

I'd forgotten that this was her first exposure to this kind of stuff. Well, her first exposure when not in immediate peril. The situation at the base inside Roosevelt's head hadn't left us with much time for sightseeing.

"Isn't it insane?" I said. "It's, like, even cooler than in the movies."

She didn't say anything back. She just stared.

"The Agency Headquarters in Minnow is even more amazing," I said.

"You've been inside the headquarters?"

"Yeah, and you'll never guess where it's located."

"I don't even know if I want to know!" she said. Her brain seemed in danger of completely overheating, so I gave it a few seconds to catch up before spilling the details.

"It's under the school."

"What? Like in a secret room in the basement?"

"No, underground. Like, way underground. Also, a bit of advice: Don't ask them too many questions about the Agency. They'll tell us what we need to know, and pretty much nothing else. They're obsessed with secrecy and stuff."

"I've noticed," she said.

Agent Blue and Agent Nineteen came back into the main compartment of the truck. Agent Blue was wearing short brown shorts, a brown shirt, and brown hat marked with the UPS logo, the standard UPS driver uniform.

"Seriously?" I said.

"Yes," he said. "Don't you think it would look suspicious for people to see someone wearing jeans and a T-shirt driving around in a UPS truck?"

"Good point," I said. "So, how are we going to even track them down?"

Agents Nineteen and Blue ignored my question. Or maybe they hadn't heard me. Instead they sat down at the computers inside the truck and started typing stuff. They seemed pretty focused, so I just took a seat at the small conference table in the center of the room. Danielle sat across from me.

"Are you sure you're ready for this?" I asked her.

"I already saved your life once today, remember?"

I grinned. "Yeah, good point."

"I still just can't believe you kept this from us this whole time," she said.

I looked down at the floor, feeling horrible all over again. "I had to," I said. "And I know you understand, deep down. We just lied to Dillon a few minutes ago."

She hesitated before responding.

"I get it, but . . . I mean, it's all so shocking and cool and unbelievable. I think I'd have found it impossible not to tell my best friends from the beginning. Especially someone like Dillon, who would be the only one to believe it. I guess I'm just not sure if I should be really impressed or really hurt and offended. Or both."

"It's more complicated than that," I said. "I really do trust you guys, that's what made it so hard for me. I wanted to tell you so many times, but if I did, you could have been in danger."

She shrugged and then smiled. "I know. But you could have at least told us when we were helping you infiltrate the secret enemy hideout at the fairgrounds."

I was about to plead my case again, but Agents Nineteen and Blue began talking. Danielle and I quieted down so we could listen in.

"What about Jake's involvement?" Agent Nineteen

said. "What does it mean? Do you suspect his mother might be involved, as well?"

"It's possible," Agent Blue said. "But I don't believe that's the case. Ms. Tyson-Gulley has never been red flagged in any of our investigations into the local community. If she's involved, she has as clean a cover as I've ever seen."

"But if so, how could Jake have been recruited?"

Agent Blue merely shook his head, then glanced up at Danielle and me.

"Do you two have any ideas?" he asked.

"Not me," I said. "We told you everything we know about him back on the mountain. What about Phil? Do you know how he could have been compromised?"

"We don't," Agent Nineteen said. "I'm going to assume it is related to the Medlock breach, but that's purely speculation."

"So how in the world are we going to find them?" I asked.

"We already know where they are," Agent Blue said calmly.

"What? How?" Danielle asked.

"There's a tracking device inside the virus receptacle, of course," Agent Nineteen said.

"Man, you guys track everything," she said. "Don't you trust anybody?"

"We can't afford to," said Agent Blue. "It's a necessary, if unpleasant, reality of the Agency's purview. Suspicion, surveillance, background checks, these things are standard Agency procedure for all our employees, targets, and assets. It's in the very nature of counterespionage and national security to trust no one and suspect everyone. It would be naive and dangerous not to."

"So you two don't even fully trust each other?" asked Danielle.

Agents Blue and Nineteen glanced at each other uncomfortably.

"Look, we're wasting time here," Agent Blue said. "So I will say one final word on this: We trust each other as much as we can within the parameters of what it means to be an agent. In this context, that's enough."

"Okay, well, let's get back to the topic at hand, then," I said, anxious to change the subject. All this talk about secrets and trust was suddenly making me really sad for some reason. "We know where Jake and Phil are, thanks to the tracking device. So, where are they?"

"Snaketown," Agent Nineteen said.

0101010101010000010100101010010101010100
101010000100101001010100101010101010101
00001...001100101010101010101010
0010...00101010100101010101001
101 ...101010010101010101010101
000...1100101010101010101010

CHAPTER 36

SNAKEPEOPLE

SNAKETOWN WAS ONE OF THOSE PLACES THAT YOU OFTEN find in areas near big tourist attractions. Like the Black Hills, which housed one of the country's most recognizable national monuments, Mount Rushmore. There was the Dinosaur Park, Bear Country USA, the Cosmos Mystery Area, the Crazy Horse Memorial, and Snaketown, among many others.

Or at least that's what Danielle told me during the sixteen-mile drive there. I'd never been to Snaketown before, since I'd never visited the Black Hills. She and

Dillon had been down here on a family vacation once, maybe six or seven years ago, but they hadn't visited Snaketown. Dillon had refused, convinced that the employees would turn out to be Snakepeople, a race of half snake, half human mutants trying to lure in reptile-loving purebred humans to use for baby food. Snakebaby food, that is.

"So we never went. Instead, we ended up going to Bear Country," Danielle said.

"And Dillon didn't have any sort of problem going to a zoo made up entirely of bears?"

Danielle shook her head and shrugged.

The agents were coming up with a plan to get the virus back, but they hadn't told us anything about it yet. All we knew was we'd have to act soon, before Phil and Jake sold it to some terrorist group, used it for blackmail, or simply released it themselves and watched the world crumble around them.

Agents Nineteen and Blue were both up in the front of the MBU discussing details as Agent Blue drove, which left Danielle and me by ourselves at the small conference table in the back. Without windows, the motion of the truck jumbling and weaving through the Black Hills was sort of disorienting. Like a slow-burn carnival ride.

A few minutes later, Agent Nineteen came back and sat across from us at the table. He looked at us evenly for a good fifteen seconds before saying anything. I got the feeling that he might be trying to assess our current mental states or something like that. Like he was giving us a full psychological evaluation just by looking at our expressions.

He smiled thinly. "I will admit," he finally said, "that there is still a lot we don't know. And, as such, our plan is littered with question marks."

"Great!" I said. Danielle smacked my arm.

Agent Nineteen continued, ignoring my sarcasm and Danielle's justifiably violent reaction to it.

"The good news is that we know the virus is still nearby," he said. "The bad news is that we still don't know what they intend to do with it. As far as we can tell, they have been sending various communications from Snaketown, but both the content of these messages and the identity of their recipients have been encrypted. The virus might already be airborne for all we know."

Danielle and I exchanged glances. This time her expression mirrored how I felt: scared, anxious, and maybe, just maybe, a tiny bit excited.

"Either way, given all those unknown variables,

there's only one option now: We must attempt to retrieve the virus immediately. Taking out the Rushmore base was likely a key move in their plan: Not only did it make it possible to steal the virus, but it completely depleted the Agency's presence for hundreds of miles in every direction. We cannot wait for reinforcements. We've got Agency Obsidian choppers en route from Minnow, but they're still well over an hour away. We also cannot wait for the enemy to make the first move. We must simply go in, now, while they're contained in this remote area, and get the virus back. Director Isadoris has given us the go-ahead. And so we're headed directly to Snaketown as we speak." He stopped to check his watch. "ETA, three minutes."

I spoke first. "And you want us to wait here and watch your backs while you two infiltrate the base, take out all the bad guys stealth-style, have a big showdown with Phil, and recover both the virus and the antidote?"

"That's perhaps a bit more colorful than we would have put it, but that's more or less what Agent Blue and I had in mind, correct. But I'd still like to review the mission with you both, since we'd like for you to monitor a few things from here."

"Sounds good to me," I said. Danielle and I both

breathed a sigh of relief. But I had to admit, deep down, I kind of felt oddly disappointed.

"Good," Agent Nineteen said, unrolling a large schematic on the table, not unlike the one that I used to infiltrate Teddy Roosevelt's head. "The reason we don't think we'll need your help is a simple matter of logistics. The decision to use Snaketown as a base or hideout is actually quite genius of them. The entire structure was built with security in mind; after all, it houses thousands of snakes, including several of the most deadly species in the world. Keeping things in and out of certain areas of the building was of the utmost importance when it was designed and constructed. Because of the building's construction, there's really only one possible way into the building: right through the front gate."

"You're joking," I said.

"You really think this is a good time for jokes, Agent Zero?" he said sharply.

I shook my head, feeling bad.

"The problem is," he continued, "the virus is currently located in a room deep inside the main building, and there are guards stationed throughout the compound."

He drew red *X*s on the blueprints with a marker to represent the guards. He marked off over a dozen, both inside and outside the compound's main building, including several on the roof. Then he circled three possible entrances into the compound.

"How do you know where the guards are?" I asked.

"A combination of satellite imaging as well as a live feed of their security camera uplink systems," he said. "As you can see, the layout of the compound and positions of the guards leave the front entrances to both the facility grounds and central building as the only viable entrances, even if we are slightly outnumbered."

"Slightly outnumbered?" I said, panic forcing the words out of my throat. "It's almost ten to one! You'll never make it! Plus, there could be more guards you can't even see. It's a suicide mission!"

Agent Nineteen nodded slowly. Almost too slowly. As if he knew very well that this was a major flaw in the plan, and yet there was nothing he could do to change that.

"Yes," he finally said. "It will be a risky mission. However, we have two key elements on our side: the element of surprise; and progressive knowledge of their defensive positions. With those two major tactical advantages, we just may be able to pull this off."

"Let us help! I can use a gun!" I said, even though I'd

never before fired a real gun in my life.

"No," Agent Nineteen said, "we just can't, in good conscience, bring you directly into such a risky mission. It's simply too dangerous."

"But we can't risk the virus getting out!" I pleaded, not even sure why I was arguing to go on such a mission so fervently. "You said so yourself. It's why you initiated the self-destruct sequence inside the base."

"I'd tend to agree with you, Agent Zero," he started, "but the advantages gained by bringing you in on the front-gate assault do not outweigh the risk factors associated with either of you getting harmed. If either of you are injured or killed, it very well may distract Agent Blue or me enough to put the whole operation at risk of failure. Given your lack of experience and training with assault weapons and tactical incursion strategies, I just don't think you'd be able to provide any real assistance. But there are several things we'd like for you to monitor from here."

I just sat there as the truck bounced along, too shocked to say much. On one hand, he was right—I didn't even have remotely close to the same training and experience as they did. But just as he said how worried he'd be about me and Danielle going on the mission, I found I was just as worried about him and Agent Blue. I didn't like the idea of them going in on their own, and there being nothing I could do about it. He was right, and yet it still hurt. So I just sat there and stared at the blueprints, once again counting the number of guards they'd face on this suicide mission of theirs.

And that's when I noticed something.

"I do have one skill to offer that neither of you do," I said, finally. "A third major tactical advantage that they'll never see coming."

"Let's hear it," Agent Nineteen said, sounding skeptical but slightly curious.

"I have experience crawling into small spaces," I said. "What if, while you guys try to enter through the front, I sneak into the compound here, then up the side of this building, and enter though this small vent on the roof?"

"But there are two armed guards right there, Carson," Danielle said, pointing to two red Xs on top of the compound.

"Yeah," I said. "But I would also have the element of surprise, and I bet there is some sort of weapon or gadget that I could use to incapacitate a few unsuspecting guards. And two attempts to infiltrate would undoubtedly be better than one, especially if one of us is discovered, as it would open up an opportunity for the other. Right?"

Agent Nineteen nodded slowly as he stared at the blueprints, likely visualizing my plan in action. He just kept nodding, not saying anything.

"And, Danielle," I said, turning, "you'll stay back here and monitor stuff like in the original plan."

"No way!" she said. "I'm going, too. You're going to need me."

I shrugged. She was probably right. And it would be nice to have help again.

"Wait here," Agent Nineteen finally said. He got up and went to the front of the truck, closing the door behind him.

"You're sure you want to come with?" I asked.

"Assuming they actually let us help, yeah, of course," Danielle said, though the look on her face completely contradicted her words. "Besides, someone will need to help you read those blueprints and navigate the ventilation system within the building."

I took a deep breath. The more I thought about it, I wasn't even sure if I was ready for this myself. Then again, did anybody ever really feel ready for a dangerous, crazy mission to infiltrate a secret enemy hideout inside a facility housing thousands of deadly snakes?

Oh, man. I'd forgotten about the snakes.

Before either of us could say anything else, the truck pulled to a stop. Several seconds later, Agents Blue and Nineteen joined us in the back of the MBU. Neither of them sat down.

"Agent Zero," Agent Blue said, "I've been filled in on your proposal. Having one student involved in all this was bad enough. Now we'd be asking that of another, while a third is also involved in a capacity we don't even fully understand. This has already gone way beyond what the Agency ever wanted or intended, and far beyond what either of us can frankly stomach. The fact is, it is happening, and now we just have to deal with that. All of that said, are you sure you'd be up to the tasks as described in your proposal, knowing very well that anyone participating in this operation might be injured or killed?"

It seemed to me that his miniature sermon was more for his own peace of mind than for Danielle and me, but I didn't say anything about that. I was exhausted, scared, nervous, yet somehow also completely wired, likely from adrenaline. It was an odd combination of feelings and emotions and I was struggling to deal with it appropriately.

Which is why I nodded and proceeded to make another terrible joke at another terrible time.

"If I do this, you should change my codename to Agent Vent," I said.

"That can be arranged," Agent Nineteen quipped back immediately.

"Okay, well, never mind that," I said. "Bad joke. The point is, I'm in."

"Me, too," Danielle said.

Agents Nineteen and Blue looked at each other, but neither said anything. Deep down, I'm sure they both realized that this was a much better plan than simply trying to sneak their way in despite being outnumbered by fifteen to one.

They finally faced Danielle and me again, and Agent Nineteen said, "Okay then, let's get to work."

0101010101010000010100010101001010101010
1010100001001010010101010010101010101010
00001010101010101001100101010101010101010
00101011010100010010010101001010100101010100
10101000010010100101010010101010101010010
0000101010101010100110

CHAPTER 37

BEYOND SNAKEDOME

WE WERE PARKED ABOUT A MILE AWAY FROM SNAKETOWN. Agents Nineteen and Blue had departed on foot to do some in-person recon on the compound, to verify the security presence and whatnot.

Which left Danielle and me sitting inside the truck alone and thinking about the dangerous and crazy mission we'd be engaging in soon. Danielle and I stared at the maps in silence, taking it all in. Memorizing stuff was her specialty. I knew that I'd be in good hands with her along. Just the same, Agent Blue had stressed the importance of us both learning the way in case we got separated or only one of us actually made it inside the vent.

I tried my best to memorize the path through the vents to the room where the virus was located, but I found myself just trying to mentally psych up for the mission. It was already evening now, and it had been a long day, to say the least. Millions of lives being at stake kept me awake, but I wasn't sure if it could do much more than that on its own.

"For all the gadgets, I really just wish there was a coffee machine on this thing," I said.

Danielle grinned at me, in spite of all the tension and anxiety crammed inside the truck with us.

"You don't even like coffee," she said.

"Yeah, but I'm tired. How about a Red Bull then?"

She rolled her eyes and went back to studying the map. Sitting right there, watching her soak up the information, I suddenly felt like with her help it would all be okay. Having a partner made the whole secret-agent thing at least ten times better.

"You've got the map down already?" I asked.

"I'm getting there," she said. "The building layout is actually fairly straightforward. At the center is this massive glass dome where over forty species of snakes are kept housed together in a tropical ecosystem. Some of the most exotic and deadly species in the world are inside, including an eighteen-foot anaconda named Gus. That dome is the keystone of the whole place. Everything else kind of branches out from there, which means it's got a series of ventilation ducts suspended from the glass ceiling from which you can get to anywhere in the complex."

"Let me guess, we're going to have to pass through the dome of snakes, right?"

Danielle smiled again. "Why? Are you scared?"

She was taunting me, but I could tell she was just as scared as I was. But maybe if we both pretended not to be together, it wouldn't feel so bad.

"Well, no, not exactly," I lied again. "I like snakes just fine. They're basically my favorite animal. In fact, I'd probably own a thousand of them if my mom would let me. I'd sleep on a bed of snakes every night. Snakeman. That'd be my nickname."

"Right," she said. "Remember that time way back when we were, like, eight years old and we were playing in the coulee behind our house?"

"No, not at all," I said, even though the truth was that

I still had nightmares about it. "I have no idea what you're talking about."

"I'll refresh your memory," she said. "You and Dillon and I were playing soccer in the coulee and then Dillon almost stepped on a snake. It was the first time any of us had ever seen an actual snake, in the wild. Do you remember what happened next?"

"Maybe," I said.

"You screamed and then ran back into the house and hid under our kitchen table crying," she said. "It took our mom a half hour to get you to come out from under the table. Eight years old, Carson."

Yeah, she was picking on me, but I knew it was her attempt to ease the anxiety. And it was sort of working.

"I don't like snakes," I said, shrugging.

"Ha!" she said. "But you know what, that was the day that I knew I wanted to be best friends with you, as cheesy as that sounds."

"Why?"

"Because you weren't afraid to actually *be afraid* of something in front of us," she said. "You weren't pretending to be something you weren't just to impress us. You weren't afraid of being made fun of. It was genuine. You were just you."

I didn't know what to say to that. I just smiled, and Danielle smiled, too.

"Well, to answer your question about the Snakedome," she continued, "it looks like all the ventilation shafts pass through there. But don't worry. We'll be high above the snakes, safe inside the metal vents, right?"

I nodded.

Agents Nineteen and Blue returned to the truck a few minutes later. They were wearing all black and held huge machine guns with scopes and laser sights.

"What did you find?" I asked.

"Good news and bad news," Agent Nineteen said.

"And more good news," Agent Blue added.

"Well, that sounds . . . uh, good?" I ventured.

They nodded and then climbed inside the truck. They were carrying two small backpacks full of gear.

"Supplies for you guys," Agent Nineteen said, setting down the bags.

"So what's the good and bad and good news?" Danielle asked.

"Well, the bad news is that we confirmed that it's very heavily guarded by security cameras and armed guards," Agent Blue said. "Including more guards near the vent than we originally suspected."

"But that's also good news," Agent Nineteen said. "I don't think they'd have the virus so heavily guarded if they planned to release it anytime in the immediate future. Not that that means we can risk waiting any longer. We've still got to move. They might be negotiating the sale of the virus as we speak."

"Okay, so what's the last bit of good news?" I asked.

"After reconning the area in person, we think a modified version of your plan actually has a slim chance of succeeding," Agent Nineteen said. "Are you ready to hash it out?"

I nodded.

Danielle seemed even more anxious to get started.

"Let's do this," she said.

CHAPTER 38

EL QUIPPO

"**W**AIT, WAIT, YOU'RE CALLING THE PLAN WHAT?" I SAID, NOT sure I heard them correctly.

"The El Quippo," Agent Nineteen repeated himself. "The Loudest Quietest Inside-Out Plan in History."

I still couldn't tell if he was joking around. This didn't really seem like an appropriate time for jokes. As if reading my mind, Agent Blue offered an explanation for the strange name.

"We just felt that, given the unusual nature of the operation, we'd give it an equally unusual and uncharacteristic name," he said.

"So what does Quietest Loudest Outside whatever whatever mean?" I asked.

"It means," Agent Blue explained, "that there will be a whole lot of loud action happening on the outside of the building. From our end it will seem like the least covert, loudest plan ever initiated. But on the inside, it might be quiet as a funeral home . . . eh, bad example, perhaps. But the point is, things on the inside, if all goes according to the plan, should go smoothly and quietly. Hopefully."

"Why attract attention, though?" I asked. "Can't we both go for stealth from opposite ends? I mean, that's what I suggested in the first place."

"Because the whole point is to draw as many guards away from the ventilation as possible," Agent Nineteen said. "To do that, we'll need to make some noise. There are four guards stationed there, not just two. We simply don't like your odds versus four armed guards. So our job will now be to draw some of them away."

"Couldn't you just plant some explosives?" I said. "That would be a good diversion."

"We could," Agent Blue agreed. "But the problem there is that random explosives detonating will *look* like a diversionary tactic."

"These guards will be too well trained for that," Agent Nineteen added. "Which is why we're going to make our frontal assault look like a stealth mission gone bad, as opposed to simply a direct frontal assault."

"If you say so," I said, knowing that they knew way more about tactical assault missions than I did. Plus, I certainly wasn't going to argue with any part of the plan intended to draw armed guards away from where I was going to be.

Agents Blue and Nineteen spent the next ten minutes laying out the plan step by step. It was essentially a more detailed version of what I'd suggested earlier on the drive here. They envisioned the operation working out like this:

Agents Nineteen and Blue would engage the building security in a massive firefight at the main entrance of the complex. It would obviously be dangerous, but there were several positions where they could stay relatively well covered. Agent Blue even mentioned something about a rocket launcher.

Meanwhile, Danielle and I would scale the perimeter fence on the southwest side of the complex using two automatic grappling hooks.

We would use the same devices to scale the side of the

main building itself, codenamed Dakota Snakehouse, to get roof access. There were presently nine roof guards including four on that side. But Agents Nineteen and Blue believed the guards would be too busy engaging their offensive attack to notice two small intruders.

Once on the roof, we'd enter the building through the largest central exhaust vent.

Using a handheld tracking device and our memory of the layout, we would follow the signal through the vents to the location of the virus.

Next, we would put on gas masks and use a canister of potent sleeping gas to incapacitate any individuals guarding the virus.

Then one of us would enter the room with the motorized grappling-hook device, gather up the virus and antidote, and exit the building the same way in which we got in.

If any of the guards also happened to be wearing gas masks, since they were themselves guarding a lethal toxic gas, then we'd also each have a small tranquilizer gun loaded with enough horse tranquilizer to take down an NFL offensive lineman in under two seconds.

No radio contact with Agents Blue and Nineteen would be maintained due to the possibility of signal interception, and so all parties could maintain the utmost focus on their mission objectives.

The rendezvous point was the UPS truck MBU, located seven tenths of a mile due east of Snaketown. The rendezvous time was precisely forty minutes after mission initiation.

"Easy peasy, right?" Agent Blue said at the end of the briefing.

"Yeah, right? I mean, what in the world could go wrong?" I said. "It's airtight like spaceman food sealed in tinfoil baggies."

"Your sarcasm is noted, Agent Zero," Agent Nineteen said. "And we can't disagree that this is an intricate plan with too many steps left open to unpredictable variables. I can't lie to you, we're as nervous as you likely are. But at the same time, the situation warrants immediate action using the resources most immediately available. The fate of the world truly depends on what we all do right now, right here. And, might I remind you, this was your idea."

"Yes, it was," I agreed. "And I'm ready to go and get this virus back."

0000101010101010101001100101010101010101010
010101010101000010100101010100101010100
1010100001001010010101010010101010101010101
00001▢▢▢▢▢▢▢▢▢▢0011001010101010101010
001▢▢▢▢▢▢▢▢▢▢001010101010010101010011
01▢▢▢▢▢▢▢▢▢▢101010010101010101010
00▢▢▢▢▢▢▢▢▢▢1100101010101010101010

CHAPTER 39

ONE SWIPE OF THE BLADE

AGENTS NINETEEN AND BLUE WERE DEFINITELY RIGHT ABOUT one thing: The outside part of the plan definitely had to be one of the loudest covert operations conducted in the history of spy missions.

The sounds of gunfire and explosions were so deafening, so present around Danielle and me as we hid in the forest behind the southwest perimeter wall of Snaketown, that even as far as we were from the action, I could almost feel every one of them vibrate inside my bones. Who knew two guys could wreak so much havoc?

Danielle and I scanned the rooftop of the main Snake-town building, codenamed Dakota Snakehouse. Before the action had begun, there were several armed guards pacing all along the south and west sides of the roof. Once Blue and Nineteen had initiated the diversion, several of them broke away to join the other guards on the perimeter while two remained behind.

As the diversion escalated, and Agent Blue began firing missiles into the compound walls, the other two guards also disappeared from view, likely to provide more backup to the others.

"I guess it's time," I whispered. Danielle nodded. "Are you ready for this? Nervous? Scared?"

She nodded again. I wasn't sure which of those she was saying yes to, but if she was feeling anything like I was, it was all three.

"Let's go," she said.

We ran from the cover of the trees to the base of the tan safari-themed wall that ran around the perimeter of Snaketown. It was at least ten feet high. Thankfully, we had two mechanized grappling hooks like the one I used back at Mount Rushmore. We fired the grappling parts toward the top, secured the motorized pulley parts to our belts, and hit the switches.

The tiny pulleys easily lifted us to the top of the wall and slowly lowered us down the other side. We hit the grip-release buttons to retrieve the grappling hook ends, ducked behind a nearby maintenance shed, and then reassessed our situation.

There was no sign of any guards on this side of the complex. We could see the top of the Snakedome sticking up above any other structure. On the other side of it, there was a particularly loud explosion and a few seconds later shards of plastic and pink cotton wall insulation came raining down all around us.

"Man, they need to be careful not to blow up the whole building."

"I'm sure they know what they're doing," Danielle said. "Come on, we should go while the coast is still clear."

We ran toward the southwest corner of Dakota Snakehouse. It was only one story, but the roof was still easily thirty feet above us. I wasn't sure what the maximum range of our grappling hooks was, but I figured it had to be at least that high. Agents Nineteen and Blue wouldn't have given them to us otherwise.

Or so I hoped.

"Come on, let's go!" Danielle shouted next to me.

With the diversion happening just around the corner,

we both had to shout in order to be heard. Danielle had already secured her grappling device to the edge of the roof above, and I did the same. Then we hit the switches and started ascending.

As the little mechanized pulleys lifted us slowly toward the roof, I dug inside my backpack for the tranquilizer gun. I wanted to be ready, just in case any of the guards had stayed behind to watch the entry vents.

But, as it turns out, we didn't need to even wait to get to the top to find out. Because when we were about ten feet from the top, a man's face peered down over the side of the roof at us. He scowled and pulled out a knife.

He slipped the massive blade under Danielle's grappling wire and cut her line with one quick swipe.

CHAPTER 40

SOMETIMES IT IS JUST LIKE THE MOVIES, REDUX (SORT OF)

WE WERE JUST A FEW FEET FROM THE TOP WHEN THE guard cut Danielle's line. So the fall shattered half of her bones. Or, I mean, I guess I should say it *would have* had I not somehow managed to reach out and snag her wrist as she fell.

I can't take all the credit, though. She also was able to grab my backpack, and our combined efforts were enough to keep her from plummeting to her demise. Or a very bad headache and six months in a body cast, at a minimum.

Once I was sure she was secure, I focused my attention back on the guard, who was already moving to cut my grappling hook wire. I had fractions of a second to act, and so I didn't even get a chance to think about what I did next. My body just kind of acted on its own.

I kicked backward on the wall just enough to get a better angle while swinging the tranquilizer gun up with my free hand. I fired a single shot just as his blade reached underneath the wire.

The small dart lodged itself in the guy's hand. He let out a surprised yell and took a step back, away from the edge of the roof. The knife tumbled down toward my face. I closed my eyes and flinched, wondering what exactly having a knife buried in your forehead would feel like and just how long it would take before I died. How much pain would I actually feel?

Thankfully, the knife merely grazed my cheek. I opened my eyes again and noticed that we were basically at the top now, the motor having never stopped pulling us up, even with almost twice the weight.

"Did the knife get you?" I asked, wiping away a bead of blood dripping down my face.

"What knife?"

"Never mind," I said. "I hit that guard with a

tranquilizer. I think he's unconscious by now. Can you crawl over me and up to the roof ledge?"

"Yeah," she said, and started climbing up my back, using my pack of supplies as a ladder. Then her knees were on my shoulders and she was able to grab the edge of the roof and hoist herself up. That's when a burst of machine-gun fire roared above me, much, much closer than the constant popping of gunfire from the opposite end of the Snaketown complex.

Danielle rolled to her left on the roof's ledge as chunks of concrete sprayed up around her. Taking a dart to the hand must not have been potent enough to completely knock out the guard. Or maybe there was more than one still up there?

My heart caught in my throat as Danielle rolled off the ledge of the roof.

At first I thought she'd been hit by one of the bullets. But she just managed to grab the ledge and keep herself from falling for a second time. My next thought, then, was that she certainly wasn't going to be able to hold on much longer.

The desperate look she gave me while dangling there confirmed as much.

She was too far away for me to reach from where I

was still hanging from my grappling hook. I'd need to get onto the roof and pull her up. But the armed guard hanging out up there certainly complicated the situation.

"Carson, please, I can't . . . ," Danielle said quietly. Desperately.

Her fingers slid on the surface of the roof's edge. She quickly adjusted her grip before she lost it entirely. Then they started sliding all over again. I knew I had maybe thirty seconds at most.

I had no clue how many darts I had left in the tranquilizer gun, but it didn't matter. I'd have acted the same way even if I were completely unarmed. I reached up and grabbed the edge of the roof with my free hand. Then I swung myself up, gun hand first, and began blindly firing random shots onto the roof as I pulled my body up and over the ledge.

My hope was that the threat of being hit again would distract the guard from firing his own weapon just long enough to give me a chance to at least get onto the roof and get a look at what I was dealing with. In the best-case scenario, I envisioned that one or more of my blind shots would actually hit the guy. Or at the very least, once I was on the roof, I'd do a cool action roll to my right and then dive back to my left, evading the spray of his machine gun while firing a perfect shot right into the center of his forehead. Just like in the movies.

But it's not always like it is in the movies. And so, of course, that's not what happened. Not at all what happened.

What happened was this:

I rolled onto the roof like I planned, but in the process of doing so lost my grip on the tranquilizer gun. While I landed (quite painfully) midroll on the hard surface of the roof, my gun clattered harmlessly across the surface, sliding at least six feet away and well out of my reach.

Not that it mattered. I landed squarely on my back and knocked the wind out of myself. I could barely breathe, let alone pick up any gun that was within reach. Which it wasn't anyway.

The guard, who had most definitely not been hit by one of my blind shots, emerged from his cover behind an air duct. He grinned as I sat up and tried to get my lungs functioning again. I wheezed as he started taking slow, deliberate steps toward me while letting his machine gun drop to his side.

"What the heck?" he said. "You're just a kid? You're the punk who did this to me?"

He held up his hand. The needle from the tranquilizer

dart I had fired earlier had passed right through his palm so that it was sticking out the other side. Which I supposed explained why not enough of the tranquilizer within had passed into his bloodstream.

What happened next was straight out of a Looney Tunes cartoon as opposed to some cool action movie. He took a few more steps toward me, but on his last step, his thick army boot landed on one of the cylindrical tranquilizer darts that I'd blindly fired onto the roof. It was made of some ridiculously strong metal and so instead of getting crushed, it rolled. His boot rolled with it and he lost his balance, flailing wildly in midair, one hand with a dart stuck in it, the other holding a heavy machine gun. The guard went sprawling backward.

Once again, I acted faster than my brain could think. I found myself springing into a somersault toward my tranquilizer gun. I reached it and had it in my hand in less than two seconds.

I rolled myself into a natural crouch and pointed, aimed, and fired off a shot, all in one single motion.

The guard had just been getting to his feet when the dart struck him. This time it hit him squarely in the crotch of his pants. He let out a scream and then dropped his gun as his hands clasped instinctively around his wounded . . . uh, *area*.

He rolled on the ground, writhing for a second or two, before the tranquilizer kicked in and he passed out.

But I didn't even have time to admire what I'd just done, because my only concern right then was whether I'd run over to the roof's edge to find Danielle still barely hanging on, or just a set of parallel scratches in the concrete where her desperate last attempts to hold on had failed.

CHAPTER 41

COUNTING STARS

WHEN I SCRAMBLED OVER TO THE EDGE OF THE ROOF, Danielle's fingers were still clinging to the concrete. They were pure white from the strain. I reached down with both hands and grabbed her forearms just as her fingers finally slid off the edge.

"What took you?" she gasped.

"Ready?" I asked.

She nodded. I leaned back and pulled her up onto the roof ledge. Exhausted, we both toppled back onto the gritty concrete roof. We just lay there next to each other for several seconds, breathing hard but not saying anything.

Even with the not-so-distant sounds of the gun battle happening on the other side of the building, the star-blanketed sky looked almost surreal. I know I talk smack about North Dakota a lot, but I forget that it does have its perks from time to time. Not many places in the world offer night-sky views like the Dakotas.

But the euphoria of having just saved Danielle's life was perhaps making it seem even better than it really was in that moment.

"Thank you, Carson," Danielle said quietly, finally breaking the silence.

"That's what friends are for," I said, sitting up. "You know, saving each other from thirty-foot plunges and maniac guards with automatic weapons. No big deal."

She managed to laugh through her shock. "Or rescuing them from a secret spy base inside of a huge stone bust of an ex-president that is about to implode, you mean?"

I laughed back and nodded. "Exactly. What good's a friend if they haven't done that for you at least once. Right?" I got to my feet and held out my hand to help her up. "Come on. Our mission's just getting started."

We ducked behind a metal air duct. Way across the roof of the building, through the glass of the Snakedome sticking up in the center, we saw guards running along the edges of the roof. They were firing machine guns out into the forest surrounding Snaketown and ducking for cover in chaotic tandem.

If any of them came back here or even looked our way for any amount of time, it wouldn't take long to spot us or figure out that something was amiss. We had to get inside quickly.

We removed the cover to the vent with a small, motorized screwdriver, and then climbed inside. We replaced the cover behind us, just in case another guard came back this way.

Once inside, we switched on tiny flashlights attached to headbands and Danielle turned on the little tracking monitor Agents Nineteen and Blue had given us. It looked a lot like a smartphone. It was basically just a little device with a touchscreen that had the blueprints of Snaketown loaded into it.

Danielle pulled up the blueprints and found the flashing red dot that indicated the current location of the virus. She studied it for a few seconds, and then looked up at me. The light from her headband blinded me momentarily.

"Sorry," she whispered.

"No problem," I said, rubbing at my eyes.

"All right, we're going to crawl for a little while, and then turn a corner and enter the Snakedome. It's going to be a pretty long crawl around the perimeter, where we'll exit through another vent. From there, it should be a straight shot to where the virus is being kept. Are you ready?"

I nodded, pretending that I wasn't worried. That I completely didn't care that in a few moments we'd be crawling through a thin metal vent above a giant atrium filled with poisonous snakes and one monster eighteen-footer named Gus. And that this flimsy vent was all that would be between me and a literal snake pit.

"Yeah, sure," I said. "Whatever. It's just snakes, right? No big deal."

0101010101010100001010010101010010101010100
1010100001001010010101010010101010101010101
00001010101010101010011001
00101011010100010010
1010100001001010010101
0000101010101010100110

CHAPTER 42

BISON APOCALYPSE

DANIELLE TOOK THE LEAD SINCE SHE HAD A MUCH BETTER IDEA where we were going than I did. The first thing I noticed once we started crawling through the vents was just how sore my knees were from having to do the same thing twice before earlier that day. Sure, crawling around in vents wasn't exactly tortuous, but the metal surfaces weren't really all that soft either. But I pushed on, knowing that we were getting close to getting the virus back and quite literally saving the world for real this time.

The thin metal vents clanked and popped as we moved. These ducts seemed less sturdy than the vents inside Teddy Roosevelt's head. Which actually made a lot of sense since those had been encased by mountain rock. Whereas these ducts probably rested on drywall and insulation, if anything at all.

I just hoped that any guards underneath us wouldn't hear it. The metal sides were definitely too thin to stop bullets. And we had literally nowhere to run or hide if we got caught.

A few minutes into our journey, Danielle suddenly stopped and switched off her headband light. I did the same without needing to ask why. There were voices below us.

Once my eyes adjusted to the relative darkness, I noticed a few streams of light just ahead of Danielle. We were about to pass over an open vent cover. The sound of voices grew louder.

"So what's next?" one of the voices said.

It was Jake.

"In thirty minutes we rendezvous with Medlock at the House of Scandinavia," the other voice said. "We'll hand off the virus to him there."

So Medlock was involved in all this after all. Somehow it didn't surprise me. Had he figured the Agency might use me again in a pinch and recruited Jake to tail me? Did he have Phil strike right before our field trip to ensure this would play out just as he wanted? I clenched both of my fists. Once again, it was my fault that we were in this predicament.

"What then?" Jake asked. "What will he do with it?"

I expected Phil to deflect the question. That's what the Agency would do with me. They'd likely say, "That's not something you need to know right now, Agent Zero." But I was wrong.

"He's going to use it to blackmail the Agency," he said. "He'll get them to provide him with money, resources, and information. The US government never negotiates with terrorists. But that's why they have the Agency: a division totally off the books. They'll give us what we want."

"How can Medlock be so sure?" Jake asked. It's the same question I would have had. "I mean, I know he used to work for them and all. But how does he know how they'll act in this situation?"

"Because they'll realize they have no choice," Phil said confidently. "The only alternative will be to sit back and watch as Medlock releases the virus at next Friday's North Dakota State Bison football game, infecting tens of thousands of people at once, ensuring a near apocalyptic loss of life. And the deaths would be on the Agency's hands. After all, they're the ones who created the virus, and it's one of their own who took it from the lab. Negotiating with Medlock will be a no-brainer."

"But he's going to release it anyway, right?" Jake said.

"Of course," Phil said. "We need the chaos to ensure that Medlock can put the rest of his plan into motion."

Why was Phil telling Jake all this? It was like they trusted him as much as any of Medlock's other agents.

"Come on," Phil continued, "let's gather the virus and get ready to make for the extraction point. The technician should have the tracking device removed by now."

"What about the guys attacking the front gate?" Jake asked as they continued walking again.

"Don't worry about them, our guards can handle themselves," Phil said as their voices faded. "In fact, I've heard one of the attackers has already been taken down."

The voices trailed off completely.

"Did you hear that?" I whispered. "One of them was hit!"

"We can't worry about that right now," Danielle said, but I could see the fear in her eyes, too. "You also heard that plan, right? They're going to release the virus, and they're heading to the lab right now to get it and take it to an extraction point. We have to get there first, Carson. If they found a way to remove the tracking device, we can't let it leave this compound."

"You're right," I said, fighting back the tears at the possibility that either Agent Nineteen or Agent Blue might already be dead.

"Let's keep going," Danielle whispered. "But keep your light off for now."

We continued crawling, making more of an effort to stay quieter this time. I trusted Danielle knew where she was going and so didn't ask questions as we pushed forward. I followed her lead when she eventually switched her light back on.

The vent shafts continued to groan under our weight, and at one point the creaks got even louder. Each move forward caused another popping dent to form under my hands and knees.

And that's what I was thinking about when the vent completely broke in half and I started falling.

The last thing I saw was Danielle spinning around as the panel beneath me gave way. I closed my eyes and waited for impact. For certain death. But it never happened.

My descent did come to a jarring stop, but it wasn't from hitting the ground. Instead, the straps of my backpack dug hard into my armpits and I found myself dangling from the broken section of metal air duct by nothing more than the loop on my backpack.

I looked down, shocked and delighted at my luck. But that feeling quickly faded as I realized I was dangling above the Snakedome. Just eight or nine feet below me were a bunch of tropical trees and plants and foliage. And below them, snakes. Lots of snakes. There weren't thousands of them piled up together in some crazy mound or anything like that. The place was a zoo, after all, and that would obviously be inhumane. But I did see several snakes: a small red one coiled up in a bush, a huge constrictor, probably named Gus, wrapped up in a nearby tree, and what looked like a black or brown cobra sliding smoothly through the brown brush directly below me.

Danielle's whisper came from above me. "Oh, no, Carson! Are you okay?"

I looked up. She had poked her head out of the section of vent above me that had not fallen down. It was still secured to the upper wall that ran along the perimeter of the glass dome. At least she hadn't fallen.

"Not really," I said back.

"I heard it break and when I turned around and saw you were gone, I thought . . ." She stopped and shook her head.

"Nope, I'm still here, just hanging around," I said, holding out my arms as I dangled from the broken vent.

"This is hardly the time for bad jokes," she said.

"That's a great joke and you know it!"

I didn't really think this was a good time for puns either. But it was the only thing distracting me from the snakes below. There really weren't many things that creeped me out. Spiders on my face in my sleep? Eh, no big deal. Fish guts baking in the sun? Not really. Giant rats eating a dead bird? Whatever. Scorpions in my shoes? Ouch, but also kinda cool. But snakes? No thanks. Refer back to eight-year-old me crying under a kitchen table at the mere mention of a harmless corn snake nearby.

"Seriously, what are we going to do?" Danielle asked, looking panicked. "Can you climb back up the vent?"

I reached behind me and tried to grab the edge and pull myself up. From the angle where I was, though, it was impossible. I was stuck there. A sitting duck for any guards who passed by.

"What should I do?" she said. "I can't just leave you here."

"You have to. Keep going and finish the mission," I said. "I'll be fine here. Once you get the virus and rendezvous with Agents Blue and Nineteen, just let them know where I am. It's the only choice we have. Someone has got to get that virus! You heard Jake and Phil back there. We don't have much time."

Danielle nodded and took a deep breath. She knew I was right. Our mission was more important than me. Or her. Or any one person, or any handful of people. That virus could literally kill billions of people over time. We had to get it back. And thankfully they'd given each of us our own gas masks and canisters of sleeping gas in our packs, so she could still complete the mission without me. It had only been a precaution, but it turned out to be a necessary one.

"Good luck, and be safe," I said.

Danielle nodded. "You, too. I promise I will come back for you, one way or another."

Then she was gone.

And it was just snakes and me.

CHAPTER 43

ELEVEN WAYS TO DIE
INSIDE SNAKEDOME

AS I DANGLED THERE, LOOKING DOWN, I BEGAN TO UNDER-stand what made Snaketown so popular. There were *a lot* of snakes. After just a few minutes, I'd seen at least seven different species. And that's a lot considering that visibility inside the glass dome at night wasn't great.

There was enough light coming from my headband, four faint yellow emergency lights posted around the dome's perimeter, and the light from the moon and stars coming in through the dome's glass panels to just make out most of what was in my immediate vicinity. But it was a lot harder to see in the shadows of the trees and bushes. The lighting created a lot of dark pockets of potential death.

A few of the snakes I saw were bundled up and immobile. But most of them were active. They were slithering around, climbing the trees, moving way more than any of the snakes I ever saw at the regular zoo or pet stores. Were snakes nocturnal? Like fish and owls and bats? It had to be the case. Unless the zookeepers here pumped them full of stimulants or adrenaline or something so they provided a better show for the tourists?

By this point, several of them had noticed me. I know that seems absurd, but I was convinced they knew I was there. I was pretty sure that snakes hunted by detecting body heat or something. And they almost looked as if they were trying to get closer to me to figure out what I was.

Needless to say, it was pretty horrifying when my backpack straps started to tear. It began with a little ripping noise followed by me lowering a few inches closer to the snake pit.

I desperately reached up behind me again, trying to find anything to hold on to. My fingers brushed against the smooth metal of the broken vent, but it was slick and there were zero handholds. There was another dull ripping noise, and then I was falling as the backpack straps tore completely. I reached up and snagged one of the straps in a last-ditch effort. And for a moment, I thought I'd saved myself. But the nylon strap wasn't particularly easy to hold on to and it slid out of my grip before I had a chance to get my other hand up to help.

Seconds later, I was sprawled out on the surprisingly soft dirt ground below. I twisted my ankle slightly in the fall, and it definitely didn't feel great. But overall, I was probably pretty lucky I hadn't broken any bones.

Especially because that would have kept me from leaping to my feet and running toward a nearby clearing where there seemed to be less plants and trees for snakes to hide in. Every step I was sure I was about to step on a deadly poisonous snake. Or a giant constrictor named Gus. Or even just a harmless small snake would have adequately freaked me out.

My first impulse was to scream, and it took all my focus not to yell uncontrollably as I ran. I also tried to keep my eyes up. If I was stepping on snakes, I didn't want to know about it.

The fifteen-yard run from where I fell to the clearing was the longest five seconds of my life. My skin crawled.

The hair on my neck tingled. I clenched my jaw so tightly that my molars ached. Snakes? Seriously?

Once I reached the clearing, I realized how much I was sweating and took off my jacket. These must have been tropical snakes, because it had to have been at least eighty degrees inside the dome, if not hotter.

I put down my jacket and then stood on top of it. Then I spun around, looking for any snakes investigating my presence. I only saw one: a green anaconda or some such massive snake. Thankfully it was in a tree at least ten or twelve feet away. Which was obviously a lot closer than I would have preferred, but considering where I was, twelve feet was better than what it could have been. Plus, a snake as thick as a softball surely couldn't move very fast. Right?

That's when I heard the last thing I expected to: human voices.

"I knew I heard something," a man's voice said. It was coming from the other side of Snakedome.

"Check out the vent," another voice said. "There's a backpack up there. Yeah, we've got intruders."

"We should report this right away."

"Wait, wait. If we go now, whoever it is might get away. We've got to find him."

"Are you kidding? I'm not going in there with all those snakes! The sign outside said there are eleven different poisonous species in there."

"Oh, come on, they're only snakes."

I realized then that I hadn't been breathing. I exhaled as quietly as I could, spinning my head around with wide eyes, still wary of snakes. Poisonous snakes. Eleven different species that could probably kill me with a single bite.

That's when I realized my headlight could lead the guards right to me. I quickly reached up and switched it off. Which only gave the snakes even more darkness to lurk in.

"Fine, let's go," the other guy relented.

"If a snake comes after you, then just shoot it, man! They ain't bulletproof."

"Yeah," the other guy said, much quieter this time.

Then the voices stopped. And I knew it was because they were inside the dome now, looking for me. They didn't want to give away their positions.

I looked up at my backpack still dangling from the broken vent. It contained all my possible weapons, including the tranquilizer gun, sleeping gas, the grappling hook, a Taser, and a few others that would have been better than what I currently had: nothing. I was an unarmed seventh-grade kid up against two grown men likely carrying real guns. In a dome filled with poisonous snakes, no less. And I was standing right near the very spot they would likely look for me first.

Just another Saturday for a secret agent, I guess.

CHAPTER 44

WHEN FEAR BECOMES
A WEAPON

LEARLY I'D BE AN IDIOT TO JUST STAND THERE WAITING FOR them to come and shoot me like a fish in a barrel. Although, come to think of it, I bet shooting a fish inside a barrel would be a lot harder than people suspect, especially if the barrel was filled with water. But that's not the point. The point is, I needed to move. Hide. Run. Something.

The fear of the snakes had nearly paralyzed me at that point. But eventually my brain was able to make my feet move, and I ran in the opposite direction as the voices. It was difficult to see where I was going without my headlight, but the yellow emergency lights still made it possible to keep from crashing into any trees or bushes inside the darkened dome.

My initial hope was to find the dome exit and then circle around to whatever door they'd entered through. But the problem with that plan was that the walls of the dome were glass. Which meant any guards walking by on the other side would easily see me. And I seriously doubted they'd mistake me for a Snakeperson.

So I didn't go all the way to the glass wall. Instead, using the curve of the ceiling above me to gauge how close I was to the edge, I stopped what I figured was maybe ten or twelve feet shy of the glass wall. I'd tried to move as quietly as I could, but I figured it was possible they'd heard me dashing through the brush.

Before moving again, I ducked behind a tree and listened. Silence. No footsteps, no voices. Then I noticed I was crouched right next to a medium-size gray-and-red snake. Its tongue flicked out, just inches from my foot.

I let out a shout and started running again. Obviously not the smartest thing to do. But cut me some slack. What would you do if you leaned forward right at this very moment and looked under your feet and saw a snake staring back? Yeah, I doubt you'd be silent either.

"Hear that?" a voice said.

"He's over there," the other responded.

They sounded farther away than they had when I'd first heard them, which meant I had put some distance between us. But that was obviously about to change. I kept moving, weaving around trees and bushes, jumping over several smaller plants. I saw multiple snakes in the dark as I ran. Some right by me, others in trees, but I did my best to ignore them either way. A snake might bite me if I happened to fall right on top of one or something. Those two guys, however, definitely would shoot me if they even saw me. And bullets were pretty much always fatal, if you could believe movies and TV shows.

So, forget the snakes.

After running and weaving my way back toward the center of the dome, I saw a spot where several trees were growing almost on top of one another. I ran toward it, this time checking for any snakes before ducking behind the lower part of a trunk. I tried to catch my breath as quietly as I could while looking around me, making sure there were no snakes within striking distance. There was one a few feet away, but it was curled into a ball, not moving.

For now.

I slowly poked my head up and looked around the tree trunk. It was hard to see very far in the dark, but after a few seconds my eyes caught some movement. At first I just figured it was another snake, but it quickly became clear that it was one of the guards.

His back was to me as he slowly crept along, his head moving side to side, scanning the environment.

I'd somehow flanked him. I wish I could say that was exactly what I'd been trying to do. But the truth was, I had just been running away from where it sounded like their voices were coming from. The flanking maneuver was just dumb luck.

But I still had no weapons. Everything that could have possibly allowed me to take down a trained adult with a machine gun was still inside my backpack hanging from a broken air duct. I didn't think I could do it unarmed, even if I did have the drop on him.

A quick search around me produced only a thin branch that was maybe three feet long and half an inch thick. It was sort of sharp on one end, but was likely too thin to actually break someone's skin before it snapped. Plus, the idea of stabbing some guy with a tree branch felt pretty brutal and barbaric. I didn't think I could do it.

Still, I held on to the stick as my eyes did one last pass around me for a weapon. And then they stopped on the sleeping snake. I kept looking at it, then glancing at my stick and back at the snake again.

The next thing I knew, I was carefully walking toward the coiled viper. My brain seemed to be fighting my actions. My feet felt like they weighed a thousand pounds. But I pushed on because it was all I had left. It was this, or face down a trained guard with a gun empty-handed.

The snake stirred as I neared, lifting its head slightly. Its dark tongue flicked out of its mouth and it took every ounce of self-control for me to not drop the stick and run screaming toward an inevitable rendezvous with several bullets. I clenched my jaw again, nearly crushing my teeth, and slowly extended the branch toward the snake.

It put up surprisingly little fight as I stuck the branch under its coiled body and lifted. It mostly just seemed curious about what was going on. I turned and made my way toward the guard, moving much faster than I would have were I holding a pillow or something harmless and not a snake. I crept up behind the armed guard and then ducked behind a bush. Taking a deep breath, I pulled the branch back and flung it forward, launching the snake into the air.

The writhing, four-foot-long snake landed directly on top of the guy's shoulders and head. He started screaming almost instantly and began running wildly across the Snakedome. I stayed behind the bush as he ran through the trees.

"What's wrong?" the other guy yelled, running after him.

The Snakeguard just kept screaming and running. Right before he moved beyond my view, I saw the snake still dangling from his face, attached to the man's cheek by its fangs. I cringed. Was that really less barbaric than impaling someone with a stick?

"Oh, man, how did that happen?" the second guard yelled.

"I don't know, it just came out of nowhere! Get it off, get it off!" he screamed.

"Your face is swelling up pretty bad," the other guy said, perhaps a little too calmly, all things considered. "Come on, let's get out of here. There's got to be antivenom around here somewhere. If someone is still in here, he likely won't last much longer. Besides, I just got word from Phil that we're evacuating."

The other guy just kept cursing and screaming. I listened as their voices faded and eventually became completely inaudible. They were definitely outside the dome now, which meant if I followed where their voices had gone, I'd find the exit. I stood up and started jogging in that direction. I had gotten no more than four steps when I tripped on a rock and fell flat on my face into the dirt.

I lifted my head and wiped away the dirt from my eyes.

And found myself staring directly into the unblinking, unflinching black eyes of a cobra.

CHAPTER 45

LAZY EYEBROWS

THE COBRA REARED BACK. IT WAS ONLY TWO OR THREE FEET from my head. I didn't watch a lot of shows about snakes, but I'd seen enough to know that cobras are lightning quick and could easily strike at this distance before I even knew what was happening.

Its hooded head was spread wide as it raised itself even higher. I knew if I tried to make a move, it would likely strike. But, to be completely honest, it certainly looked like it was eventually going to strike either way.

A bead of sweat trickled down my face and across my

nose. It eventually fell off and landed in the dirt under my chin. More sweat began streaming down into my eyes. It was so hot. The salt burned. Stupid eyebrows. Not doing their job very well, that was for sure.

I tried to slowly ease myself up so I was at least on my knees and not lying on my belly. I was maybe halfway up when the snake finally struck.

It moved so fast, I barely had a chance to register what was happening. One second it was just hovering there, reared back and ready to defend itself. And a fraction of a second later its face was zooming in right at mine, fangs first.

In that brief moment, I had just enough time to realize that there was no way I'd be able to dodge it. This was it; I was about to get bitten right in the eyeball by one of the most deadly breeds of snake in the world.

But then a hand came flying in out of nowhere and grabbed the snake's head just a few inches from the tip of my nose.

I looked up and saw Agent Blue holding the snake as it writhed and curled in panic. He effortlessly flung it across the dome in one smooth movement. It landed on the branches of a tree a good thirty feet away and immediately squirmed its way toward the trunk. Then he reached down and helped me to my feet without saying a word.

There was a sudden flash of movement in the corner of my eye and I took an instinctive step backward. Agent Blue's eyes went wide and he looked down at his leg.

A small yellow snake had latched itself on to his calf. Agent Blue didn't grimace, or yell out in pain. He quickly reached down, dislodged the snake's fangs, and then tossed this one away into the depths of the Snakedome.

"Come on, let's get out of this awful place," he said.

I followed him as he jogged toward a door hidden along a small patch of concrete at the edge of the dome where it connected to the main Snaketown building on one side. He opened it and then followed me into a dark hallway.

We went through another door and found ourselves in a tourist exhibit area on the other side of the Snakedome's glass. There were benches and placards on podiums detailing several of the species of snakes to be found within the dome.

"We should check to see if that snake was poisonous," I said, starting toward the information platform.

"No, we don't have time," Agent Blue said. "Come on, follow me."

"I heard one of you was hit— Is Agent Nineteen . . . is he . . ." I couldn't bring myself to finish.

"He's fine," Agent Blue shot back over his shoulder. "Come on, move!"

I followed him through the empty corridors of Snake-town, wondering why we hadn't seen any sign of guards, and wondering a whole lot of other stuff as well. But Blue was moving too quickly for me to have time to ask any questions. Even with the limp he had developed.

Then suddenly we rounded a corner and were face to face with Agent Nineteen and Danielle. She smiled slightly when she saw me, then, just as quickly, the smile was gone.

"What's wrong?" I asked. "Did you get the virus back?"

Nobody spoke. Danielle answered by simply shaking her head.

The mission had failed.

CHAPTER 46

LEGGO MY LEG DOUGH

"**W**HAT HAPPENED?" I ASKED.

"Come on," Agent Blue said. "I'll explain it as we walk. There's no time to waste."

And so we followed him as he kept moving through Snaketown back toward the front gate.

"Phil managed to escape the complex with the virus moments before Danielle arrived at the holding room," Agent Blue said. "Shortly after we fully engaged the perimeter following our 'failed' covert attack, the guards withdrew."

"They likely received an evacuation order," Agent Nineteen added.

"So at that point, we entered the complex and headed toward the signal from the virus's tracker," Agent Blue continued. "It was on the move by then. We found Danielle along the way, after she saw us through an open vent and alerted us to her presence. She told us what happened to you and we went immediately to the dome, knowing that the virus was already out of the complex and moving faster than we'd be able to on foot. Which brings us to here."

Agent Blue finished his recap just as we got to the Snaketown parking lot.

It had taken Danielle and me too long to get to the virus. They'd managed to escape with it and it was my fault. Again.

"But we can still follow them," Agent Blue said, holding up the tracking device. "According to this they're currently heading east on Highway Sixteen."

"No," I said.

"What?" Agent Blue asked.

"I mean, we can't track them," I said. "Danielle and I overheard Jake and Phil talking when we were in the air duct. Phil said they found a way to remove the tracking device."

"No, that's impossible," Agent Nineteen said. "It can't be removed."

"I'm telling you, they found a way," I said. "Danielle heard it, too."

"It's true." She nodded.

"They also said they were currently on their way to meet up with Medlock," I added. I proceeded to quickly fill them in on what we'd overheard as we continued moving through the Snaketown parking lot toward a lone car near the back.

"Then we absolutely need to follow this signal," Agent Blue said. "We have to stop them before they rendezvous with Medlock. Once that happens, we'll be too late. Even if we know where they're releasing it, there's no guarantee we'd be able to stop them in as uncontrolled an environment as a football game. If we have any hope of stopping them, it's right now."

"That's what I'm saying, though," I said. "That can't be the right signal. They said they were meeting Medlock at some place called House of Scandinavia."

Agent Blue stopped as we reached the car, a silver Ford Fusion. He looked again at the virus GPS tracker. Then he shook his head.

"You must have misheard them," he said. "This says it's headed east on Sixteen, but House of Scandinavia is west on Highway Sixteen, just past Bear Country."

"You have to trust me," I pleaded. "I know I heard them right. What if they were able to remove the tracker? That signal is a diversion." I pointed at the tracker. "You ask me to trust you two all the time. Now I need you to trust me. We have to go the other way. We have to get to House of Scandinavia before they all escape."

Agent Blue exchanged a quick look with Agent Nineteen before facing me again.

"If you're wrong, then we all lose," he said quietly.

"I'm not," I said. Danielle nodded, agreeing with me.

"Then let's go west—come on," he said, motioning toward the car.

"Whose car is that?" Danielle asked.

"No idea, but it will be a lot faster than the MBU," Agent Blue said.

"You've got keys?" I asked.

"We've got this," Agent Nineteen said, holding up the same device he'd used to steal a car from the Mount Rushmore lot earlier that day.

It was only then under the parking lot lights that I

finally noticed the blood dripping onto the pavement next to Agent Nineteen's shoes. He was holding his stomach and his clothes and hand were soaked in blood.

He swayed slightly on his feet, but stayed standing.

"What happened?" I asked, hearing the panic in my own voice.

"I'll be fine. Come on, we're wasting time," Agent Nineteen said as he shuffled toward the car.

By this point, Agent Blue could barely walk himself, favoring the leg that had been bitten. Agent Blue used the device to unlock the car. He helped Agent Nineteen into the backseat as best he could with his poisoned leg. Then he crouched by the driver's-side seat and had the car running within seconds.

Agent Blue sat down on the pavement and tore open his pants leg at the seam. I cringed. His leg was red and so completely swollen that it looked like a giant blob of dough. It actually would have looked pretty funny in almost any other situation. And gross, of course.

"Ugh, what happened?" Danielle asked.

"He was bitten by a snake," I said.

"I don't think I'll be able to drive," said Agent Blue. "And he'll be no help." He pointed back at Agent Nineteen, who was slumped against the door, passed out. He was definitely still alive, because his shallow breath was creating little clouds on the inside of the window. But I truly wasn't sure how long he'd hold on. Tears began to well up again, and I forced them back down.

I didn't understand how the two agents could be so unconcerned over each other's wounds. If Danielle were shot or bitten by a poisonous snake, I'd be freaking out. And that's when it dawned on me. The mission was still on, and they knew better than to waste time worrying over each other's injuries. We still had a job to do; we had to stay 100 percent focused on getting the virus back. There simply wasn't time to ask one another if we were okay or how badly things hurt or to worry about whether or not our friends would die. This was why they were as good as they were. If it were me sitting there looking at a nearly dead Danielle, I'd probably be nonfunctioning and the virus would be as good as gone.

"Who's up for driving?" Agent Blue asked.

I looked at Danielle.

"I think you got this," she said to me.

She was right. I was the best option; she didn't even like driving bumper cars. It was up to me. The problem—and it was a big one—was that my only experience behind the wheel had been earlier that year when Olek and I had driven that car and crashed it into a ticket booth at the fairgrounds. Not exactly the best first attempt. I had to hope I'd get the hang of it this time.

0000001010101010101010010011001010101010101010101
001010101010101000010100101010101010010101010
010101000010010101001010101001010101010101010
000001010101010101001100110101010101010100101
100101011010100010010101010101010010101010100
0101010000100101001010101010101010101010100010
00010101010101010010010

CHAPTER 47

SAILOR! TO THE MOON
WITH YE!

"**D**ON'T WORRY, IT'S JUST LIKE DRIVING A GO-CART," AGENT Blue said. "You've done that before, right?"

I sat behind the wheel and nodded. Agent Blue was up front in the passenger seat. Danielle was in the back with a still-passed-out, and still-bleeding, Agent Nineteen. She put pressure on his wound according to Agent Blue's instructions, and looked at Agent Nineteen with a sad and worried expression.

"Okay," Agent Blue said. "Gas pedal on the right,

brake on the left. That's it. You can do this, Carson. You have to."

I nodded again, pressed down on the gas pedal, and we were off. Or, we should have been. But instead the car just sat there as the engine roared.

"Ease off the gas," Agent Blue said. "Put the car into drive first."

I shifted the gear stick to *D* like I'd seen my parents do plenty of times before. And then, for real, we were off. The going was slow and awkward at first. The car jerked forward as I switched between the gas and the brake.

"Which way to the House of Scandinavia?" I asked as we pulled up to the parking lot exit.

"Take a right," said Blue. "That will put us on westbound Highway Sixteen."

I did as instructed.

"They have such a big head start—how will we catch them in time?" I asked.

"They likely don't want to attract the attention of the police," Agent Blue said as I gradually got comfortable taking the car over fifty miles per hour. "Plus, they have no idea that we know where they're really headed. As far as they know, we're following the tracker signal."

The Black Hills highway was winding, which made

the drive more terrifying than it should have been. The rain that just happened to start when I got behind the wheel certainly didn't help either. Several times the car skidded several feet left or right as the tires lost traction on the increasingly slippery pavement.

"Just take it easy," Agent Blue said. "If we crash, we'll never catch them."

I nodded and eased off the gas.

We didn't pass many other cars along the way, which made sense considering that it had to have been eight or nine at night by that point. Plus, there wasn't exactly a ton of residential housing out in the forest. And with the tourism season mostly over, the whole area was rather vacant.

As I got a bit more comfortable behind the wheel, Agent Blue finally turned around to check on his partner. I glanced over and saw his normally stolid and emotionless face destroyed with worry and fear. It was one of the more unnerving things I'd seen all day, and let me remind you that it had been an insanely crazy day involving poisonous snakes, mountain climbing, an imploding secret base, machine gun fire, and more.

"How is he?" Agent Blue asked, grabbing his leg and wincing at the effort of turning around in his seat.

"I don't know, not good," Danielle said. "But the bleeding has stopped. I think."

"He's going to make it," Agent Blue said, likely more to himself than anything. "He's going to make it. He's taken ten bullets in his career. They've never stopped him before."

Ten bullets, seriously? I did my best to ignore him. Driving a car for the first time in sleet on winding mountain roads was hard enough as it was without worrying about my mentor dying slowly in the backseat.

A short time after we got on the highway, we turned a corner and spotted red taillights up ahead in the dark.

"I think that's them!" Danielle said.

"How will we know?" I asked.

Agent Blue looked at the tracker with an annoyed expression and then tossed it on the floor between his feet.

"There's no way we can know for sure," he said. "Just keep your distance, we don't want to tip them off."

"But how will we know it's them if we can't get closer?" I said.

"Carson, trust me," he said. "They'll know they're being tailed if you get too close."

"How?"

"Does it matter?" he said sharply. "They will know—trust me, I've done this before. Now ease off the pedal!"

I glanced at him. He was clearly keeping something from me, and his eyes were wide and sweat poured down his face. He kept shaking his head rapidly and muttering things under his breath as if trying to shake away a voice inside his head. He clearly wasn't himself; the snake's venom was making him delirious. I wished he'd just tell me what he was thinking. Phil didn't have any problem bringing Jake in on what was happening back at Snake-town. Why couldn't Agent Blue trust me now? I made an executive decision right then and there and pressed down on the gas pedal.

Agent Blue rolled his head to the side and groaned, not seeming to notice.

"Carson, what are you doing?" Danielle said as the speedometer passed eighty miles per hour. "He said to stay back!"

"I know what I'm doing," I said.

As if to perfectly punctuate how wrong that statement was, there was a flash ahead of us and then a bullet hole appeared in the upper right corner of the windshield and cracks spiraled out from it. I flinched instinctively and the car spun out of control. Danielle and I screamed as the left side of the car lifted into the air, and for a second I thought for sure it'd start rolling down the hillside.

But by some miracle, the car spun to a stop just off the left side of the highway.

"I told you to stay back," Agent Blue shouted. His face was pale and sweaty, and he looked barely conscious. But he still managed to yell at me loudly. "If we had just followed them to the rendezvous point and not tipped them off, we could have captured them and Medlock all at once!"

I hadn't considered that. If he just had told me his reasoning I might have actually listened to him.

"Come on, get this thing back on the road!" he said. "Now we have no choice but to try to intercept them. No doubt they're contacting Medlock as we speak to come up with a new plan now that they know they're being tailed."

The car was still running and I tested the gas pedal. The tires spun in the mud under us but slowly the car inched forward and then there was a squeal as we got on the paved road. I turned back onto the right side of the highway and resumed the pursuit, pressing the gas pedal almost all the way down.

"But how did they know it was us?" I said, desperately

looking for justification for my just blowing our chance to nab Medlock. "I mean, they wouldn't just shoot at a random car, right?"

"They must have recognized the car," Agent Blue said. "It was the only one in the Snaketown parking lot."

We rounded a curve, and then once again their red taillights were visible in front of us. More muzzle flashes came from the side windows, followed by popping noises. Several holes appeared on the hood of the car. This time I held steady, knowing that at this speed, one jerk would crash us. We'd never be that lucky a second time.

"Keep your heads as low as you can," Agent Blue said, straining to get each word out as sweat poured down his face. "Try to catch up, Carson."

"What are you going to do?" I asked.

"Shoot back," he said as he rolled down the window, filling the car with a rush of cold air and rain.

Agent Blue extended his arm out the window and started firing shots at them with his handgun. The sharp blasts of the gunshots almost caused me to swerve off the road again.

Another crack appeared in the windshield right near where my head was. I gulped. The good news was, whoever was driving the car ahead was also having a tough time staying on the road while going this fast in the sleet.

Agent Blue fired two more shots as we got closer to the car.

One of his bullets must have hit a tire, because suddenly the car veered off the road and right through a massive chain-link fence on the side of the highway. Then it smashed through another fence before finally coming to a stop at the base of a large tree.

"Pull over there!" Agent Blue pointed at the fence with the SUV-shaped hole in it. "We'll have a picnic. Did you bring jam? The blueberry kind, I mean. Not the other one . . ."

"What?" I asked, pulling the car over.

"I think the venom is making him hallucinate!" Danielle said.

"Venom! Venom was voiced by Azaria . . . or was it someone else?" Agent Blue mumbled. "I don't remember."

"What is this place?" Danielle asked, studying the double layers of barbed-wire fence illuminated by our headlights.

Agent Blue pointed up through the car's sunroof and said, "Berenstain Bears!"

We looked up at a sign looming above us. It read:

WELCOME TO BEAR COUNTRY!

There was a picture of a massive bear next to the words.

Great, first snakes and now bears. What were the odds?

I looked at the SUV for signs of movement. It had hit the tree pretty hard. Hard enough to crunch the front end of it like an accordion and smash one of the passenger-side windows. A body lay draped over the hood, having crashed through the windshield.

"What now?" I asked.

"I don't know," Danielle said, sounding truly scared for the first time. "I don't know what to do."

"We're on our own now, clearly," I said, trying not to let the fear show in my voice. "Should we go after them?"

"We have to, right?" Danielle said. "We have to get the virus back."

"What if the vial broke open in the crash?" I asked.

"Crash course!" Agent Blue mumbled. "You have to go. Get the Romero . . . you know, he's always inconsistent about the meaning of the, uh, you know . . ."

Agent Blue kept mumbling, but I stopped listening because one of the SUV's passenger doors opened and two dark silhouettes emerged, black against the nearby billboard sign's light.

They started running.

"I can't go," Agent Blue said in a rare moment of clarity.

I looked down at his leg and then had to look again. And again. If I hadn't looked at least three separate times, I never would have believed what I was seeing. His leg was so swollen now that it basically filled the entire space between the passenger seat, floor, and dashboard. It was like some kind of puffy marshmallow. Or something. I'd never seen anything like it. There was no leg down there anymore, just a massive blob of swollen flesh. And his face was a shiny mass of sweat and pasty skin.

"We have to get you to the hospital!" I said.

"No, this is too important," he said. "Here, take the Cheez Whiz."

He held out his gun. I took it carefully. It was much, much heavier than I expected.

"Agent Blue," I said. "I'm so sorry I didn't listen to you. I didn't know."

"It's okay," he said. "I should have told you why. You're an agent. It doesn't matter now. Go! Get the virus back. The world's Pop-Tarts are counting on you. And so are the elk. Or at least, they'll be lawyers. But they still want to win."

"I'm going, too," Danielle said, and we both got out of the car. The sleet hit my face, and the woods were lit creepily by the SUV's flashing hazard lights. This was all my fault. If I had just listened to Blue, we might have been taking Phil and Jake and Medlock into custody by now.

I took one last look back at Agent Blue. He gave me a thumbs-up and a smile. Then he saluted me and said, "Sailor! To the moon with ye!"

I would have laughed but I was pretty sure he didn't have much time left.

"We have to go—they're getting away," Danielle said.

"Okay." I tried to cock the gun like they do in the movies, but I didn't really know how. "Let's go get the virus back."

0101010101010100001010010101010010101010100
1010100001001010010101010010101010101010101
00001... ...0011001010101010101010
0010... ...0010101010010101010101001
101 ...1010100101010101010101
000 ...1100101010101010101010

CHAPTER 48

THREE COUNTDOWNS IN
ONE DAY IS THREE TOO MANY

THE FIRST THING WE DID WAS APPROACH THE CRASHED SUV cautiously. It was empty aside from the body draped over the hood on the driver's side. It was some guy I didn't recognize and there was clearly nothing that anybody could do for him now. And so we started running in the direction of the two figures who had gotten out of the SUV moments before.

It didn't take long for us to discover that they had crashed right into the part of Bear Country where the grizzly bears were kept. It was dark, but the light from the star-filled sky and moon was just bright enough for us to make out dark, furry shapes lying in shallow holes and man-made fake caves off the side of the road, attempting to stay away from the rain.

I saw at least one bear poking his massive brown head out of a shelter near a small man-made pond. All the commotion from the SUV crash probably woke them up, and now they were eyeing the gaping hole in the fence, which they'd likely waltz right out of before too long.

But as with the snakes, none of that mattered. We needed to focus on getting the virus back. Bears or no bears.

We'd only run maybe thirty yards when a voice suddenly called out from behind us.

"Stop right there!"

We complied. There was something about the command in the voice that told us all we needed to know. The man was armed and had a bead on us.

"Turn around," he said. "Slowly, of course. And you'd be smart to drop that gun as well."

I let the gun fall from my hand and clatter to the ground as we turned. Phil stood near a tree maybe fifteen feet away from us. His handgun was pointed right at me. He was grinning, but when he saw my face, the grin faded.

"You?" he said. "You should be dead. How is this possible?"

"I've got friends," I said.

"What do you mean by that? Ah . . . you know what? Never mind." He waved his free hand in the air. "I don't care. As we speak, my associate is making his way up to that hill over yonder with the virus, and we'll be meeting with an evacuation vehicle in fifteen minutes. You two will make a nice addition to our growing cache of bargaining chips. But first, a question, and I want the truth. How did you know to follow us this way?"

"We overheard you talking to Jake inside Snaketown," Danielle said.

Phil nodded slowly. And then he sighed.

"Of course. You snuck quietly into the base while the other agents assaulted the front gate. Clever."

"You're never going to get away," I said. "We have back-up coming right behind us."

"I seriously doubt that." He raised the gun. "If you did, they would have met you at Snaketown. Now, come with me."

"Wait!" I said.

Surprisingly, he did.

"Who are you?" I asked. "Why are you doing this? I just don't get it."

"What is this, some terrible action movie?" Phil scoffed. "Why would I waste my time explaining my actions at all, let alone to two kids?"

"But why would you betray the Agency?" I asked again. "Your partners? The government?"

He paused. But then something gave way and he scowled.

"You should know why," he finally said. "Jake told me all about how the Agency made you lie to your best friends, while it consistently withheld information from you. Doesn't that make you mad?"

It did. A little. It had since I started working for the Agency. But it still didn't make me mad enough to ever think about doing what Phil was doing. At least, I hoped not.

"It does, doesn't it?" Phil said. "Well, imagine fifteen years of that. Of never being trusted. Of knowing you're under surveillance, even when you're in the bathroom or going to the movies. To not even know the name of the agency you work for! It's ludicrous. To be treated like that is demeaning. We're supposed to trust the Agency, to trust that they are always doing what's right. But how can we trust them when they don't show the slightest trust in us?"

I was speechless. What he was doing was wrong, there was no question about it. But the things he was saying . . . They were all things I'd thought about myself. And it did make me wonder whether I'd still be able to overlook those things so easily after fifteen years of it. I had been an agent for only a few months and it was already getting to me.

"No!" he shouted. "No! Trust is a two-way agreement. Now, Mr. Medlock—he does trust me. He trusts all his associates, completely. He runs his operations transparently. Whatever you want to know about his plans, you know. It doesn't matter what you *need* to know. Do you have any idea how refreshing that is?"

"But, killing millions of people," Danielle said. "Trust isn't worth millions of innocent lives, is it?"

"Think about it," he said. "Your best friend told you dozens of lies to your face because the Agency ordered him to. What kind of world is it that we lie to one another constantly? With such ease that we sometimes don't even realize we're doing it? You tell me, what are trust and honesty worth?"

"Not this!" Danielle shouted.

"Well, we'll just have to agree to disagree on that point," he said. "Anyway, we need to move, time is of the essence."

He steadied the gun and motioned toward the woods.

I froze, unsure what to do next. Phil's words had jumbled up everything in my mind. But before I could decide what to do, I heard a whine. It was high-pitched, yet guttural, kind of like a cross between a dog's bark and a cat's meow. And it was coming from directly above Phil.

"What now," he muttered and looked up at the tree next to him.

There was a small baby bear slung over a branch. It looked like it had maybe been asleep up there until we'd woken it. It let out another moaning whine. It wasn't quite a roar. It sounded more like a cry for help.

"How cute," Phil said, turning back to us.

And that's when the baby bear's mother rose up behind Phil from out of the darkness. At full height, it towered above him. Its brown fur bristled as it let out a gut-wrenching roar.

Phil's eyes went wide and he spun around to face the bear. That's when the bear struck at Phil with a massive paw. The gun flew from his hand as he fell to the ground. I quickly picked up Agent Blue's gun and pointed it at the bear as it loomed over Phil.

"What are you doing?" Danielle asked.

"We've got to stop this," I said. "If the bear kills him, the virus is lost. We have no idea where Jake is, or any other bad guys who might have been with them. And besides, even given everything we heard right now, I'm not going to let a bear kill him right here!"

I turned back to the fight. The thing was, I didn't really want to shoot a mother bear that was just trying to protect her cub, either. The bear roared again and batted at Phil's body. It didn't strike him very hard, but the bear was so large and powerful that Phil's limp body rolled across the ground several times as if it had been hit by a car.

He moaned and tried to get to his feet. The bear knocked him back down with another swipe of its paw.

I aimed the gun at the bear. I had to do it. I closed my eyes and pulled the trigger.

Click.

I pulled the trigger again, expecting a bang.

Click.

It was empty. I tossed the gun aside. Then I noticed a second bear approaching us from the side. It was another large brown bear.

"Uh, we should go, Carson," Danielle said.

"But, Phil!" I said. "The virus!"

"We have to try to find the other person we saw. There's nothing we can do for Phil now!"

She was right. As we spoke, the mother bear grabbed Phil's pant leg in her mouth and dragged his lifeless body into the shadows behind her.

I nodded at Danielle.

We started walking backward slowly, away from the two bears. The second bear watched us go and for a moment I was certain it was going to chase us. But then it turned its attention away and headed back into the darkness. As we kept walking, the baby bear climbed down the trunk of the tree. It would have been adorable if we were normal kids here on vacation.

But that was not important.

What was important was getting to that virus before it was released. Phil had said someone was making his way to an evacuation vehicle with the virus in fifteen minutes. That meant we had only about ten minutes before the virus was gone. If Medlock got his hands on it, we'd never find it before it was too late. Our only chance was to catch this guy before he escaped.

Great. Yet another countdown to disaster.

Wasn't two in one day enough?

0010101010101010000101001010100010101010
0101010000100101001010101001010101010
0000010101010101010011001 0101
1001010110101000100101 0100
0101010000100101001011 010
CHAPTER 49

TEN MINUTES(ISH) AND COUNTING

DANIELLE AND I RAN TOWARD THE GROVE OF TREES PHIL HAD pointed out earlier. We reached it a lot faster than I expected, even with us being careful to avoid what looked like possible bear dens in the mostly open hillside around us.

By the time we got there, we likely had only a few minutes to spare.

Most of the land within Bear Country was stripped of trees, which made sense when you considered it was a drive-thru bear zoo and people would want to see bears and not brown shapes hidden by trees. But this particular spot had been left intact, I guess to give the bears at least a little bit of a natural forest habitat.

"Come on out," I said to the patch of dark trees.

"Where's Phil?" a voice said from within the shadows. A kid's voice. Jake's voice.

"Jake?" I said.

There was a long pause.

"Carson?" he finally said. "How are you still alive?"

"That doesn't matter. Just come on out so we can talk," I said.

"Where's Phil?" he asked again.

"He won't . . . ," I started, and then stopped and considered whether that was the best thing to say.

"He's not coming," Danielle finished for me, apparently not as worried about how Jake might take the news. Apparently, she'd had it with telling lies.

"Well, it doesn't matter," Jake said. "An escape vehicle is going to be here in a few minutes, and there's no way you're getting this virus back before then."

CHAPTER 50

SO MUCH FOR THE
RULES OF COUNTDOWNS

"**W**AIT!" DANIELLE SHOUTED. "JAKE, IT'S DANIELLE."

"I don't care," he said. "You never liked me anyway."

"At least come out and talk to us first," she said. "We won't try anything, I promise."

"Yeah?" Jake scoffed. "What good is a promise from you?"

"Who told you that?" I said. "Phil? Medlock? Well, you got the wrong idea. It's not like they say it is. The information the Agency withholds is for our own protection. It's not about lying, it's about security. The secrets are meant to protect us from what we shouldn't know."

"I'm tired of lies, too," Danielle said. "So to that effect, yeah, I admit I never really liked you. But it was justified. You've been deceiving us all along. So you should be able to recognize a real promise when you hear it. We just want to talk. We won't try anything funny. Trust me."

"Whatever," Jake said from the darkness. "I don't care about that stuff. All I care about is helping my dad fix things. He'll fix everything. He's the only one I trust."

I exchanged a look with Danielle, who looked just as confused as I did. As far as I knew, his dad was just some big-shot orthodontist who made tons of money but was never around and so bought Jake whatever he wanted to make up for never being there for him.

"Your dad?" I said. "Is he not a real orthodontist then?"

"No, not him!" Jake said. "Dr. Gulley isn't my real dad. I mean, he thinks he is, but he's not. Which is all for the better."

"Come on out so we can talk about this face-to-face," Danielle said. "We aren't even armed. Surely you can see that's true from in there."

Jake didn't answer for what felt like hours. And I

was convinced that the little backstabbing psycho had just released the virus or something. But then a hand emerged from the shadows beneath the trees. A hand holding a small vial.

Then Jake stepped completely out into the clearing, holding the virus up in the air.

"If you take one step toward me, I swear I'll smash this thing," he said. "Though, if I were you, I'd run now while you still can. Medlock and his men will be here in three minutes to get me, and once they're here you'll both be in serious trouble."

"We'll take our chances," I said.

"So, if Dr. Gulley isn't your dad, then who is?" Danielle asked.

"Why should I tell you?" Jake said.

But at the same time, I think he had to know that we had a decent guess as to who his real dad was.

"It's Phil, isn't it?" I said, growing more and more uneasy knowing Phil's fate. "I thought you guys had similar smiles."

"No, it's not Phil." Jake scoffed as if that was the worst person who could be his dad.

If it wasn't Phil, then who could it possibly . . .

"Medlock," I said quietly. "Mule Medlock is your dad?"

"Yeah," Jake said, clearly proud. "Medlock is my real dad. And the Agency tore him away from me when I was just a little kid. He was the only one who ever cared about me. My mom and Dr. Gulley, all they care about is things and money and how everyone else perceives them. But Medlock actually cares about *me*. He cares about everyone. He just wants to fix the world."

It was some sob story. But I didn't point out that there were dozens of kids at our school who didn't have parents at all, let alone all the money and stuff that Jake did. Yeah, maybe his situation wasn't the best, but it also could have been a lot worse. Nobody had a perfect life. Then again, I definitely didn't want to antagonize him, not while he still had the virus. So I said nothing.

"Where's Phil?" Jake asked. "I told you something, now you tell me."

"That's not important," I said. "What matters is that he's not coming back and he won't be able to punish you for doing the right thing and giving us the virus."

"You killed him!" Jake shouted, pointing a finger at us.

"No, we didn't," I said. "I promise!"

"Oh, yeah?" he said. "Oh, well, Carson promises me,

so it must be true. Yeah, Carson never lies. What good is a promise from Carson Fender, the kid who flat-out lies to his best friends about important things on a daily basis? Huh?"

He sort of had me there.

"You lied worse than I did," I said.

"So? I'm not making any promises right now," he said. "I never claimed to be an honest or good person."

"We didn't kill Phil," Danielle said bluntly. "The bears did."

"Bears?" Jake said, looking around.

He seemed to be truly disoriented. How could he not have realized he was in the middle of an open-cage bear zoo? There were literally bears everywhere. Then again, most of them were sleeping, mostly out of sight, in the darkness and shelter away from the rain and sleet. But still.

"Yeah, we're in Bear Country," I said.

Jake seemed shocked for a few seconds, and then he shrugged it off. "It doesn't matter. My dad should be here any second now. I'm telling you, this is your last chance to get away."

"When were they supposed to be here?" I asked.

Jake looked at a small device in the hand not holding the virus. His face fell a little bit and worry flashed across his eyes briefly.

"They'll be here," he said.

"They're not coming," I said. "Your dad just left you here. He abandoned you. How much can he really care about you?"

"He wouldn't do that," Jake said, shaking his head.

"You know as well as I do that if he were coming, he'd already be here," I said.

Danielle took my lead and added, "Now you can do the right thing. There's still time to be the hero instead of a villain."

"It's your choice," I said. "You can make the right one right here and now."

I held out my hand for the virus.

Jake didn't say anything. Instead he seemed to search for the answer in the dirt at his feet. Then in the stars above him. Then he looked at Danielle, and then at me in turn while fighting off tears. I was sure he was moments away from giving in. Then he did something I truly never expected him to do. I had honestly believed we would be able to talk him down. But we'd clearly failed.

"If my dad isn't here, then there's a reason for it," he

said quietly. Too calmly. "And so if he isn't here to carry out his plan, then I will."

Jake lifted up the vial containing the virus and then threw it as hard as he could onto the hard ground in front of him.

0000101010101010100110010101010101010101
910101010101000010100101010010101010100
101010000100101001010101001010101010101010
900010 0011001010101010101010
9010 0010101010010101010010
101 CHAPTER 51 101010010101010101010
900 1100101010101010101010

CHAPTER 51

YOU RUINED IT!

IN THE EXACT MOMENT IN WHICH HE THREW THE VIAL ONTO THE ground, I saw it. I saw it in his eyes: He had completely checked out as a real person. We never had a chance to talk him down. Jake had clearly lost all his marbles. If he ever had any to begin with.

And now the world was over.

Or was it?

Instead of shattering and instantly releasing the virus into the air like we'd all expected, the vial merely bounced into the dirt, landing a few feet away from Jake's sneakers.

"Jake, no!" Danielle yelled, perhaps a little late.

But it was still definitely a better reaction than mine. Which was to just stand there and gape at the vial. Jake probably took the most active and drastic next step of all of us. He took a step forward and then started stomping on the vial repeatedly.

That's what finally kicked me into action.

I ran forward and dived at him. My shoulder slammed into his chest and we both went flying backward toward the trees. I landed on top of him and then rolled off immediately. I glanced up and saw Danielle picking up the vial.

In that split second that I'd looked away, Jake had gotten to his feet. And so by the time I looked back he was already in the process of kicking me in the ribs. I didn't have time to dodge or block it.

His kick caught me squarely in the side and pain erupted where his foot had connected. I rolled away and groaned. But in a fraction of a second he was on top of me, bringing his fists down wildly and indiscriminately. Which probably helped me out a lot since he connected very few punches with anything too vital, like my nose or eyes.

"Why did you do that? You ruined it!" he shouted. "You ruined it!"

At the same time I became vaguely aware of the sound of a helicopter nearby. Then a bright spotlight was on us. Jake looked up at the sky. The light got brighter and wind whipped around us as the helicopter lowered.

At first, I wasn't sure if the chopper was Agency backup or Medlock. But then Jake jumped off me and started running away. There was no way he was escaping. I was done with chases. Done with countdowns. Done with all of this today. I sat up and took off my shoe. Then, without really thinking about it too much or even really trying to aim, I threw it at Jake.

The shoe flew through the air like a perfectly spiraling football and connected pretty squarely with his head. He flew off his feet and then slammed into a tree. I flinched the way people do at scary parts in horror movies, or when watching people fall in YouTube videos.

"*That's* how to throw," I said to him as he rolled lazily on the ground in dazed pain.

I climbed to my feet just as the helicopter touched

down in an open spot within Bear Country. Several people climbed out of the cabin, their hair blowing wildly under the helicopter blades.

All three wore suits. One of them ran toward Jake. I saw him crouch down and put on handcuffs. Another of them ran back toward where the car we'd hijacked was parked with Agents Nineteen and Blue still inside and hopefully still alive.

The third man who exited the helicopter was more a giant beast of mythical proportions than a simple human being. He almost looked at home in Bear Country. And he walked directly toward Danielle and me.

"Agent Zero," Director Isadoris said, "did you secure the Romero Virus?"

I pointed at Danielle. "She's got it."

Danielle handed him the vial. He put it inside his coat rather calmly, all things considered. As if he were merely putting away a handkerchief after blowing his nose or something. Then he smiled at me.

He didn't question who Danielle was or why she was there. He didn't yell at me for almost blowing the whole thing again. Twice. He just smiled. After a few moments, he finally spoke again.

"Nice work, you two. You saved a lot of lives," he said. "But I bet you're both ready to get out of here and back to Minnow, North Dakota, yes?"

He was right. For the first time in my life, I was actually excited to be going back to Minnow, North Dakota.

"When can we leave?" I asked.

0000010101010101010100011001101010101010101010101
0010101010101010000101001010101001010101010
010101000010010100101010100101010101010
0000010101010101010100110011010101
10010101101010001001010100
01010100001001010010

CHAPTER 52

QUESTIONS

"**I**T'S REMARKABLE WHAT YOU KIDS DID," DIRECTOR ISADORIS said. "Remarkable."

It was almost twenty-four hours later and we were back in Minnow. Miles underground, inside Agency Headquarters, to be precise. Danielle and I sat across from Director Isadoris in his office. But we still didn't have any answers. The last twenty-four hours had been frustrating to say the least.

After we'd told Director Isadoris about Jake being Medlock's son and their planned rendezvous at House of

Scandinavia, he'd dispatched several agents in search of Medlock. Then he'd arranged for us to be brought back to the field trip group. I don't know what the Agency said to Mr. Gist and Ms. Pearson to convince them that Jake and Mr. Jensen, aka Agent Blue, were both fine despite the fact that they'd be traveling back separately from the group. But whatever it was, and whoever said it, it apparently worked. We saw the Crazy Horse Memorial the next morning, and then rode back to North Dakota on the bus like hardly anything weird or unusual had happened at all during the trip.

And it was torture. To have to endure a ten-hour bus trip, just sitting there wondering if Agents Nineteen and Blue were okay or dead or alive but still not really okay, was awful. Not knowing if the Agency ever found Medlock at the House of Scandinavia. Not to mention the billions of other questions I had.

Danielle seemed to be handling it slightly better.

But either way it had been kind of a nice distraction to have Dillon pestering us both for answers of our own regarding where we'd disappeared to the second time. Listening to his various theories as to where we'd gone almost distracted me from my own burning questions.

Almost.

Then Sunday evening had rolled around and my family was at the table eating dinner. We had individual chicken potpies that night, one of my favorite meals. Except that on my third bite I got a mouthful of something that wasn't chicken, or vegetables, or crust. I discreetly took the slip of paper from my mouth and unfurled it under the table.

Meet us at the school track at 7:45 p.m.

Sometimes it was best not to think about how the Agency did their thing. You slept easier that way.

After dinner, I told my mom I was going to Danielle's to work on our field trip journals and headed to the school track. I was surprised to find Danielle there waiting as well, having gotten a similar message in her chili.

Director Isadoris met up with us a short time later and then escorted us personally down into Agency HQ. Danielle was flipping out the whole time, of course, being that this was her first time inside the secret base located miles underneath the school.

And that brings us to here, at Agency HQ, sitting across from Director Isadoris in his office. With no answers still to any of my questions. And no real information regarding what exactly was going on.

"You're both heroes," he said. "Truly."

"Well, it was mostly luck," I said.

"No, it wasn't," he said firmly. "Well, maybe some luck. But being an agent isn't about having access to secret information, or being an expert with weapons. It's about knowing what to do in a situation while under pressure. And by that estimation, you've proven yourself to be legitimate field-agent material. The country owes you both a serious debt of gratitude."

"Except of course for the fact that I let Medlock get away by not following a direct order," I said. "You didn't ever find him, did you?"

Director Isadoris shook his head, but he was still smiling.

"It's okay. Don't be so hard on yourself," he said. "We need to work on that here at the Agency anyway. While full transparency in our operations will of course always be impossible, I definitely think there is room for improvement on our end. Ultimately, you felt the need to make a judgment call and were simply wrong. It happens to all of us from time to time. You trusted your gut—that's what the best agents do. Your gut won't always be right, of course, but trusting your instincts is largely why you've already been such a great asset to us. Was it a missed opportunity? Maybe. Maybe not. But we got the virus back and that's what matters most. That was ultimately your mission, and so you still succeeded in the end."

I nodded, feeling better about it than I had since it had happened.

"If it wasn't for Carson, we would have gone completely in the wrong direction to begin with," Danielle said.

"Precisely," Director Isadoris agreed.

"What about Agents Blue and Nineteen?" I finally asked, overcoming the fear that I would be given an answer I didn't want to hear. "Are they okay?"

"They're fine," he said, but then held up a hand to interrupt himself. "That is, they're not dead, if that's what you're wondering. Agent Nineteen suffered several serious bullet wounds, but he is in stable condition in our medical wing and should make a full recovery. He's remarkably resilient, almost invincible at times, it seems. Agent Blue will also live, but he may never regain full use of his leg again. If we're able to save it at all, that is. It's still too early to tell."

"Oh, man," I said, feeling especially bad that he'd been injured saving my life and then I'd gone ahead and repaid him by disobeying an order a few minutes later.

"They still have their lives, don't they?" Director Isadoris said. "And Medlock doesn't have the virus. As far as missions go, I'm prepared to call this one a success."

I nodded and then forced a smile. He did have a good point: It was just awesome that they both were going to live. It definitely could have turned out worse for them. For all of us, really.

"You have more questions?"

I nodded.

"Fire away," he said. "Pardon the expression."

CHAPTER 53

ANSWERS

"WHERE'S JAKE?" I ASKED.

"He's in our custody in a secure Gray Site," Director Isadoris said.

He said nothing else. I obviously had no chance of finding out exactly where he was, not that I really wanted to know what a Gray Site was, anyway.

"What will happen to him?" Danielle asked.

Director Isadoris shrugged. His shoulders were so massive that the shrug looked like two tectonic plates grinding together. I half expected an earthquake to follow.

"It's hard to say. We have confirmed through DNA tests that he is in fact Medlock's son. And I have to admit, I'm a little embarrassed that Medlock had a son while he was stationed here in Minnow who we weren't even aware of. But it may give us a tactical edge that we haven't had yet, of course depending on how much Medlock actually values his son. It's certainly a complicated situation if nothing else. As of right now, his mom and legal father, Dr. Gulley, think he was picked up by a park ranger in the Black Hills after trying to purposefully run away from home while on the trip and is currently being treated at a mental hospital in South Dakota. His mother, surprisingly, did not question the situation or seem to care that much. She's apparently a very busy woman. Keeping up that facade in the long term will prove difficult, but it's something we've had to do many times before, so we'll manage."

"What about Phil, did he, uh, make it or whatever?" I asked.

Director Isadoris shook his head slowly.

"Oh," I said. "What about any of the guards at Snaketown? Can we find out where Medlock is from them?

Or if anyone within the Agency besides Phil has been turned?"

We'd told Director Isadoris everything we'd found out that night about the plan and Medlock's involvement before they brought us back to the field trip group. He hadn't seemed particularly surprised by any of it.

"Dead men tell no tales, so to speak," Director Isadoris said. "And all the survivors got away, unfortunately. That said, we have a few leads from examining the few materials left behind at Snaketown and inside their getaway vehicle."

Danielle and I waited for him to elaborate. When it became clear to him that we were waiting for more information, he eventually did provide it. Sort of.

"You understand," he started, "that I have to be careful how much I share. For national-security purposes, of course. That said, given how much you've already done for us, and in light of the circumstances and the need to try to be better about keeping our agents informed, I will say that we do have several leads to follow regarding Mule Medlock's whereabouts. And, as for other potentially turned agents, a few names have been identified, yes. Along with the revelation that Medlock has at least one more spy operating within your school. Another student spy."

"Really?" I asked, stunned. "There's another enemy agent operating inside my school?"

Director Isadoris nodded slowly. "And we may have to ask for your help again in identifying who it is. But don't worry about that just yet, at least not until we're able to gather more information."

"One thing that keeps bothering me is," I said, "even after blackmailing you, Phil said Medlock's plan was to release the virus anyway. Why would he do that? How could he benefit from a near-global catastrophe?"

"Look, we're getting into some deep water now," Director Isadoris said, "so I'm going to have to end this conversation here. But let me assure you that Mr. Medlock remains a very active and real threat to this Agency and this country. And we fully intend to stay on top of the possible threats he may or may not be behind."

"That's it, then, no more questions?" I said.

"I'm sorry, Carson, no," he said. "But there is one more thing. Danielle, in light of your excellent service to this Agency, we'd like to offer you the opportunity to be added to our nonofficial list of agents, right alongside Agent Zero. Is this something you'd be interested in?"

Danielle took a lot longer than I expected to reply.

And her answer was also not what I thought it would be, considering she was usually the responsible one of our group.

"Of course!" she said with a grin.

"In that case, your new codename is Atlas," Director Isadoris said. "Welcome aboard, Agent Atlas."

CHAPTER 54

JUST ANOTHER BORING MONDAY

MONDAY MORNING AT SCHOOL, I EXPECTED THINGS TO JUST go back to normal. And they did. In their own way. I guess. Because, you see, for me a normal school day usually involved spending time in Mr. Gomez's office getting yelled at. And when a hand gripped the back of my neck almost immediately after I entered the building that morning, it seemed that that's precisely where my day was headed.

I looked behind me.

Mr. Gomez scowled. "My office, Mr. Fender, now!"

He said nothing as he marched me down to his office, never taking his hand off my neck. He wasn't gripping it painfully hard, but there was definitely enough muscle behind it to know that it'd be best for me to not resist him and just go along with it.

He sat me down and then took his own seat across the desk from me. Mr. Gomez spent several seconds just glaring at me before saying anything.

"Does signing a contract mean anything to you, Carson?" he asked. "Anything at all?"

I'd actually completely forgotten about that thing. You know, with the whole climbing-a-mountain, infiltrating-a-secret-Teddy-Roosevelt-science-lab, almost-getting-imploded, breaking-into-an-enemy-agent-lair, almost-getting-shot-and-falling-to-my-death-several-times, facing-down-a-roomful-of-poisonous-snakes, taking-out-an-armed-baddie-with-said-snakes, getting-in-a-high-speed-car-chase, getting-flanked-by-an-armed-psycho-in-a-bear-den, watching-a-bear-maul-a-man, and then tracking-down-a-deadly-virus-that-would-have-onset-the-apocalypse-thing, I sort of had forgotten about that little disciplinary contract I'd signed.

"Um—"

"Apparently nothing," he said. "Your actions have

clearly said as much. I let you go on this field trip in good faith, and what do you do?"

"I—"

"You will not talk!" Gomez shouted, pointing a finger at me. "It's my turn now. That was a rhetorical question. You'd know what that means if you ever bothered to do your homework. What you do is you disappear not once, but twice from the group for hours at a time. And you take a good student down with you!"

I assumed he was referring to Danielle here. If only he knew that she delighted in the pranks as much as I did. Not that I'd ever rat her out. I just sat there and listened.

"You know what this means, right?" he asked.

There was a long pause.

"Right!" he shouted.

"Oh, am I, uh, supposed to actually answer this one?" I asked.

"It means," he said, his snarl stretching into a smile, "that I finally get to do what I've wanted to do since your first week here at my school."

I slumped forward in my chair and nodded.

"Yes, you signed a contract," he continued. "You can't fight it this time."

I opened my mouth to finally speak. That's when the

door to his office burst open and several men in black suits and sunglasses stormed inside. My first reaction was to duck and hide. After the last two months, I was almost used to this sort of thing.

But they moved right past me and toward Mr. Gomez instead.

"What is the meaning of this?" Gomez shouted.

One of the men held out a badge.

"Mr. Gomez, I'm Agent Loften, National Security Agency," he said. "You're under arrest on suspicions of treason, terrorism, espionage, and activities detrimental to US national security."

My jaw swung open and I looked at Mr. Gomez in shock. He met my stare, but said nothing.

Yeah, just another boring Monday at Erik Hill Middle School.

ACKNOWLEDGMENTS

I'd like to thank all the people that most authors usually thank in this section. Y'all know who you are. And Jeff. I want to thank Jeff. For his vital contribution to this series. The gratitude may be delayed but is still well deserved. Also, it never hurts to give a little shout-out to frosting, for usually being the best part of cake. I'm deeply in love with you, frosting.

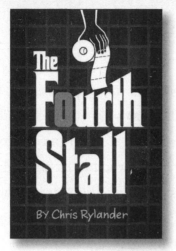